FROM NIZAMI'S DIWAN:

حدیث عاشقی بر من رها کن
تو لیلی شو که من مجنونم ایدوست

unleash upon me the saga
of being in love

o friend, be my layla
for i am majnun

The Story of
Layla and Majnun

The Story of

Layla and Majnun

by Nizami

Translated from the Persian and edited by
Dr. Rudolph Gelpke

English version in collaboration with
E. Mattin and G. Hill

Final chapter translated from the Persian by
Pir Zia Inayat Khan and Omid Safi

~Sulūk Press
Richmond, Virginia

Published by Sulūk Press
112 East Cary Street | Richmond, Virginia 23219
sulukpress.com

English translation ©1966 Bruno Cassier (Publishers) Ltd.
Reprinted with permission by Omega Publications

Final chapter of Omega Publications edition translated by Pir Zia
Inayat Khan and Omid Safi ©1997 Zia Inayat Khan and Omid Safi
Verse from Nizami's Divan translated by Pir Zia Inayat Khan and
Omid Safi
Cover photo from Persian manuscript c. 1590, courtesy of the Arthur
M. Sackler Gallery, Smithsonian Institute, Washington D.C.

Interior artwork courtesy of the national Museum in New Delhi, India,
with special thanks to Dr. Daljeet, Director of the Painting Department

Cover design by Sandra Lillydahl

Printed on acid-free paper

ISBN 9780930872526
ebook ISBN 9781941810408

Library of Congress Control Number: 2011925355

Printed and bound in the United States of America
by Sheridan Saline

CONTENTS

EDITOR'S NOTE

The *Preface* by Rudolf Gelpke is an abridged version of the *Postscript* published in the German edition, Manesse Bibliothek der Weltliteratur, Manesse Verlag, Zurich 1963. This appeared also as a *Postscript* in the English edition published by Bruno Cassirer in 1966, and the 1978 American edition published by Shambhala Publications.

Manuscripts of Nizami's *Layla and Majnun* vary significantly. Some versions introduce a character named Zayd, whose love for his cousin Zaynab is juxtaposed to Majnun's love for Layla. These manuscripts feature the final chapter as presented here, in which the heavenly fulfilment of Majnun and Layla's love is witnessed by Zayd in a dream. Following Wahid Dastgerdi's critical edition, Gelpke left these verses out of his translation, dismissing them as later interpolations. Other notable scholars, however, have regarded this material as authentic. It is likely that Nizami reworked his own poem at a later date, to lift the melancholy mood of the original. As Peter Chelkowski observes of Zayd's vision, "The opportunities it offers for love's consummation certainly heighten the drama and poignancy of its renunciation."

For further discussion, see Peter Chelkowski, *Mirror of the Invisible World: Tales from the 'Khamsa' of Nizami*, Metropolitan Museum of Art, New York, 1975, pp. 66-68; and, in Persian, Barat Zanjani, ed., *Layli o Majnun-i Nizami Ganjavi*, Intisharat-i Danishgah, Tehran, 1990, pp. 15-30.

TRANSLATOR'S PREFACE

AMONG the legendary love stories of the Islamic Orient that of Layla and Majnun is probably the best known. The two lovers live up to this day in poems, songs and epics of many tribes and nations from the Caucasus to the interior of Africa, from the Atlantic to the Indian Ocean.

Are these legends based on truth? Has this Bedouin youth Qays from the North-Arabic tribe of Amir, named Majnun (Madman), ever lived and suffered for his Layla? We can not be certain, but there are good reasons to believe that he did, probably in the second half of the seventh century A.D., somewhere in the western half of the Arabic peninsula, about 500 years before A.D. 1188 (584 H), the year in which the Persian poet Nizami wrote his poem. Nizami was the first to make use of all the traditional versions, widely dispersed and greatly varied in detail, which he shaped into one great narrative poem.

Thus the theme of Layla and Majnun acquired a new importance far beyond the narrow frame of local Arabic lyrics. Many later poets have imitated Nizami's work, even if they could not equal and certainly not surpass it; Persians, Turks, Indians, to name only the most important ones. The Persian scholar Hekmat has listed not less than forty Persian and thirteen Turkish versions and the Nizami editor Dastgerdi states that he has actually found more than 100: 'If one would search all existing libraries,' he says, 'one would probably find more than 1,000.' Even modern love stories are often influenced by Nizami.

The reason for this far-reaching influence is to be found in the fact that Nizami far surpasses all his predecessors and imitators. This is today generally accepted. The Egyptian scholar M. Gh. Hilal in his book on *The Development of the Majnun-Layla Theme in the Literatures of the Orient* (Cairo, 1954) concludes that it was Nizami who transformed the local legend into a work of art of general and timeless value; the Persian A. A. Hekmat, who in 1941 published a prose version in Teheran, compares the work with Shakespeare's *Romeo and uliet* and Jan Rypka in his *History of Iranian Literature*—the latest and most important work in the field—says: 'The result... shows the hand of a genius.' The Russian orientalist, I. J. Kratshkovskij, the first to collect the early Arabian sources, points out that, owing to Nizami's work, Majnun has become a leading figure in many other literatures.

The scarcity of translations into European languages is partly due to the lack of a reliable Persian text which was for the first time constituted from about thirty manuscripts by Wahid Dastgerdi in his edition of *Nizami's Collected Works* (Teheran, 1935). The text is accompanied by an indispensable commentary. Since then 'Layla and Majnun' has been translated into Turkish (by A. N. Tarlan, Istanbul, 1943) and into Russian (by P. Antokolskij, Moscow, 1957). Earlier part-translations, for instance the English version by J. Atkinson (London, 1836), published 1oo years before Dastgerdi's Persian edition, must now be considered as out of date. Even the quotations given in E. G. Browne's standard work *A Literary History of Persia, vol. II*, 6th edition (Cambridge, 1956), in A. J. Arberry's *Classical Persian Literature* (London, 1958), and in H. Masse's *Anthologie Persane* (Paris, 1950) are taken from parts which Dastgerdi has shown to be worthless additions by later editors.

Nizami had not chosen his subject himself, he had been commissioned by a Transcaucasian chieftain, Shervanshah, and confesses in one of the prefaces that at first he was by no means enthusiastic about the idea. This is hardly surprising to anybody who knows the ascetic aridity of the early Arabic sources which he was supposed to follow. But Nizami, while preserving the main facts, made many important additions: the scene in the garden, Nawfal's attack against Layla's tribe, her refusal to consummate her marriage, Majnun's rule over the animals, the visit of his mother and his uncle, the mother's death, the story of the youth from Baghdad, the death of Layla's husband, as well as the fables and meditations, are either not to be found at all in the Arabic sources or only in rudimentary form. It must, of course, not be overlooked that these early sources were not concerned to produce a work of art. Their object was to collect the verses allegedly written by Majnun, adding textual and factual commentaries, and to publish them together with notes about the author, his name, his origin and his life. Nizami was the first to make the Bedouin poet the centre of a poetical rendering of his story; the factual details provided by the earlier editors are for him only the basis for his own work. The only worthwhile comparison would be one between the Arabic poems preserved under Majnun's name and those Persian verses which Nizami and the more important of his successors (Maktabi, Djami, Hatefi) have put into Majnun's mouth, even though the Arabic poems have to stand on their own while the Persian ones are supported by the context of the whole epos.

It is interesting to observe how Nizami preserves the Bedouin atmosphere, the nomads' tents in the desert and the tribal customs of the inhabitants, while at the same time transposing the story into the far more civilized Iranian world. The aridity and harshness of the surroundings are framed, as it were, by beautiful descriptions of the starred sky and the rising sun, or the deepest secrets of the human soul, in a language unbelievably rich with most precious images. In the Arabic sources the background is nearly empty. Nizami frees the story from the limitations of a merely accidental event by lifting it to an altogether higher spiritual level and enriches it by his love of colors, scents and sounds, by embellishing it playfully with jewels, flowers and fruits. In one of the prefaces he says that because of the magic power of his diction he was called 'The mirror of the Invisible' and kept 'the treasures of two worlds in my sleeve'—those of the visible and the invisible ones. Majnun's father becomes 'a Sultan of the Arabs' and is at the same time 'like Korah the Wealthy'; Layla walks in a rose-garden under cypress trees where nightingales sing in the bushes; Majnun talks to the planets in the symbolic language of a twelfth-century Persian sage; the encounters of small Arabic raiding parties become gigantic battles of Royal Persian armies; and most of the Bedouin talk like the heroes, courtiers and savants of the refined Iranian civilization.

Far more important than the dramatic events of the story is the inner meaning of the work whose stage is Majnun's soul. 'What we mistake for a padlock to keep us out we may tomorrow find to be the key that lets us in' and 'every leaf in the book of fate has two pages; one is written by man, the other by Fate.' Whatever this poet touches becomes transparent and reveals its hidden meaning.

To his Arabic biographers Majnun is suffering from an illness, a broken man who has lost his way, to be reproached, pitied or derided. Nizami understands the three elements of the traditional Majnun—his love, his insanity and his poetical genius—as three aspects of one, indivisible unity. Only when he is driven out of the paradise of his early love does Majnun become both insane and a poet. Insanity and poetical genius are two expressions of the same state of mind, of a soul estranged in the world of men. And the same people who reproach, pity and deride Majnun because of his insanity, memorize and admire his poetry. Has the tragic ambiguity of the artist's position in the world, the paradox of unbounded desire in a limited body, ever been described more aptly?

On the other hand, it would be wrong to consider Majnun's and Layla's fate as 'tragic' in the western sense of the word. That there could be no fulfilment of their love on earth is a foregone conclusion for Nizami's mysticism. His Layla states clearly that, in the religion of love, close intimacy is perilous. This conception is similar to the spirit which in Europe moved the Troubadours—though only for a short time, while in Persia this age-old tradition has left its mark on all classic literature and even today is not dead but lives on like a spark under the ashes.

If, therefore, our lovers' sufferings are not 'tragic,' they must also not be interpreted from a point of view of conventional morals. The Persian mystical poets have never been puritans! The lovers' grief breaks through the limitations of human nature, enabling them to become free of their 'Self' which is tied to the transitory world. Death is the gate to the 'real' world, to the home which our wandering soul desires, and the poet reveals this truth in brilliant, ever-changing metaphors: the light-giving candle sheds bitter tears; the oyster suffers because of its pearl; the ruby longs to be freed from the rock in which it is hidden; the fading rose becomes a drop of precious rosewater; Majnun eats 'the eater in himself,' overcoming hunger, egoism and possessiveness, and crushing the 'bazaar' of sensual lust—to become the King of Love in Majesty. Not that everybody could reach this exalted state simply by falling in love: 'Inconstant love,' says Nizami, 'remains but a toy of the senses and perishes like Youth.'

Layla, loving and beloved, is, next to Nizami's Shirin, one of the most touching and delicate figures in Persian literature. No doubt she is meant to be a monument of the poet's beloved wife, Afaq ('Horizons'), who died early. Her character is perhaps best described in Layla's last words to her mother, one of the most moving episodes in our epos.

This English version of Nizami's work is, of course, not a literal translation, although it comes often very near to it. Apart from the different prefaces and the poet's postscript, which have been left out, it is based on those 3600 verses (out of more than 4000) which in the opinion of the Persian editor Dastgerdi can be accepted as genuine. His text (2nd edition, Teheran, 1333/1954) is the only authoritative one.

In some cases I had to take liberties. It is not always possible to follow exactly in a prose version Nizami's very concise poetic language. It must also be remembered that the author wrote for a very small circle of highly educated readers at the courts and in the towns of Iran in the twelfth and thirteenth centuries. Today even well-read Persian readers find difficulties in understanding the work without using an extensive commentary such as the one provided by Dastgerdi.

Some descriptions had to be shortened, as, for instance, that of the starlit sky under which Majnun prays, since this requires a specialized astrological and astronomical knowledge. Sometimes the complicated sense of a single verse had to be rendered in several sentences.

I began working on my prose version in Persia in 1958. I am well aware of the fact that in spite of all my efforts it remains inferior to the original. At least I can say it is based on a careful study of every word of Nizami's poem.

R. Gelpke

PREFACE TO 1997 EDITION

I emanated upon thee a force of love
that you might be fashioned according to my glance.
Qur'an, XX.39.

High romance blossomed in the cool shade of nascent Islam as 'manliness,' the rugged code of the desert, yielded to "udhri love,' a tender-hearted chivalry inspired by platonic eros. In the refined emotion and chaste forbearance of such legendary Bedouin 'martyrs of love' as 'Urwa bin Hizam, Jamil, and Kuthayyir 'Azza—poets who, "when loving, die"—pure love took its stand, prefiguring the courtly love of the *Fedeli D'amore* in the West and the Sufi 'School of 'Ishq' in the East. But the axial figure in this revolution of the heart was Qays bin Mulawwah, called Majnun—'the Madman'. Naked among the beasts, deliriously singing his love for Layla (whose name means 'Night'), Majnun became the sovereign 'Emperor of Love'.

Who was the 'Madman of Layla'? The Russian orientalist Krachovski has made a strong case for the lovelorn poet's real existence in western Arabia in the latter half of the seventh century. Yet the melange of stories and verses associated with Majnun frustrates the gaze of hard history. Al-Jahiz (d. 868 C.E.) complained, "People have not left any poetry said by any poet about any (girl called) Layla without attributing it to Majnun." Even the poet's proper name varies in the early accounts. Absorbed in the beauty of his beloved Layla, Majnun seems to have transcended his own biography and become the rubric for a whole gamut of lyrics and episodes betokening the madness of separation-in-love.

As the quintessential romantic fool, haunting the arid wastelands of the 'World of Images,' Majnun is a deeply resonant and rhetorically potent archetypal figure. In the rhapsodies of oral traditionists and storytellers (*rawis*) from Umayyad times to the present day, Majnun features as an endearingly pathetic antihero crushed between the claims of society and the claims of the heart. For the belletrists and aesthetes (*adibs*) of Islamdom, the love-crazed poet epitomizes the ideals of emotional sensitivity and fidelity. Highlighting Plato's theorization of love as a "divine madness" (*junun ilahi*), the psychology of 'udhri love recognizes Majnun's madness as an erotico-mystical condition rather than a pathological one. Presumed insane, the 'Madman of Layla' is said to have protested, "Love is greater than madness." Unlike the poets, soothsayers, and madmen of the pagan 'Heroic Age,' it is no jinn which possesses Majnun, but the incomparably more overwhelming force of pure love.

To the Sufis, Majnun represents the perfect devotee of the 'Religion of the Heart'. In the fervor of his passion they discern a semblance of the Qur'anic maxim, "the faithful are ardent in their love for Allah" (2:165). Ardor in love (*ashadd al-hubb*) became "ishq' in the parlance of Hallaj (d. 922), who was crucified for uttering "I am the Truth" (*ana al-haqq*)—just as, mystics believe, Majnun was to finally pronounce, "I am Layla." It was probably in the ecstatic sermons of Hallaj's friend Shibli (d. 945), a frequent inmate of madhouses, that the romance of Layla and Majnun first took the shape of a spiritual parable.

Since those early days in Baghdad, Layla and Majnun have occupied a hallowed place in the mythopoetic universe of Sufi lore. In his book of profound meditations on 'ishq, the *Sawanih*, Ahmad Ghazali (d. 1126) suggests that it was not family politics but Majnun's inability to remain conscious in the presence of Layla that kept the tragic lovers apart. Ghazali's brilliant disciple, the mystic martyr 'Ayn al-

Quzat (d. 1131) speaks of Layla's beauty as bait in a trap set out by the Eternal Hunter to snare Majnun's heart and make it a steed for love. Through the pedagogy of human love the heart is prepared for divine love, and ultimately for the vision of God unveiled. In his *Jasmine of Lovers*, the 'Doctor Ecstaticus' of Shiraz, Ruzbihan Baqli (d. 1209) explains this alchemy of 'ishq as an apotheosis of the subject, rather than the object, of love. He writes:

> Love is the stirring of the essence, the excitement of the soul, the melting of the heart. In the sweetness of discovery, the beloved harmonizes with the lover. It is for the beloved to arouse longing, and for Majnun to be the ardent lover (*'ashiq*). The state of Majnun is that of ardent love. He reaches the point where he becomes the mirror of God, and God makes an ardent lover of whoever looks into him.

It is said that when someone tried to dissuade Majnun from his obsessive love of Layla, arguing that she was really rather plain, Majnun replied, "My Layla must be seen with my eyes." Let us now borrow Majnun's tear-soaked, bloodshot eyes and look on the ethereal beauty of Layla...

Zia Inayat Khan

I

ONCE there lived among the Bedouin in Arabia a great lord, a Sayyid, who ruled over the Banu Amir. No other country flourished like his and Zephyr carried the sweet scent of his glory to the farthest horizons. Success and merit made him a Sultan of the Arabs and his wealth equalled that of Korah.

He had a kind heart for the poor and for them his purse was always open. To strangers he was a generous host and in all his enterprises he succeeded as if good luck were part of him, as the stone is part of the fruit—or so it appeared to be.

Yet, though respected like a caliph, to himself he seemed like a candle, slowly consuming itself without ever spreading quite enough light. The heart of this great man was eaten by one secret sorrow; he, who otherwise possessed everything he desired, had no son.

He had remained childless. What did glory, power and wealth mean to him, if one day they would slip from his hands, without an heir to receive them? Was the corn fated to wither, did the branch have to die? If the cypress tree fell, where would the pheasant build his nest? Where would he find happiness? Where shade and refuge?

He only is truly alive, who in his son's memory survives his own death.

Thus the noble man brooded and, the older he grew, the greater became his desire. Yet for many years his alms and prayers were in vain. The full moon which he so eagerly awaited never rose in his sky and the jasmin seed which he sowed would not germinate.

Still the Sayyid was not content to bow to his fate. For the sake of one wish yet unfulfilled he thought but little of everything else that heaven had granted him. That is how humans are made! If prayers remain unanswered, do we ever reflect that it may be for our good? We feel sure that we know our needs, yet the future is veiled from our eyes. The thread of our fate ends outside the visible world and what today we mistake for a padlock, keeping us out, we may tomorrow find to be the key that lets us in.

Much, of course, can happen in the meantime. Our hero desired the jewel he did not possess, as the oyster nourishes its pearl, so he prayed and clamored until in the end God fulfilled his wish.

He was given a boy, who looked like the smile of a pomegranate, like a rose whose petals have opened overnight, like a diamond which transforms the darkness of the world into sheer light.

Delighted, the happy father opened wide the door of his treasury. Everyone was to share his happiness and the great event was celebrated with shouts of joy and words of blessing.

The child was committed to the care of a nurse, so that under her watchful eye he should grow big and strong. So he did, and every drop of milk he drank was turned in his body into a token of faithfulness, every bite he ate became in his heart a morsel of tenderness. Each line of indigo, drawn on his face to protect him against the Evil Eye, worked magic in his soul.

All this, however, remained a secret, hidden from every eye.

Two weeks after his birth the child already looked like the moon after fourteen days and his parents gave him the name of Qays.

A year went by and the boy's beauty grew to perfection. As a ray of light penetrates the water, so the jewel of love shone through the veil of his body.

Playful and joyful, he grew year by year a carefully protected flower in the happy garden of childhood.

When he was seven years old, the violet-colored down of his first beard began to shimmer on his tulip cheeks and when he had reached his first decennium people told the story of his beauty like a fairy tale. Whoever saw him—if only from afar—called upon heaven to bless him.

II

OW the father sent the boy to school. He entrusted him to a learned man to whom distinguished Arabs took their children, so that he should teach them everything of use in this world. Instead of playing, they were now to study in earnest and if they went a little in fear of the strict master, there was no harm in that.

Soon Qays was one of the best pupils. He easily mastered the arts of reading and writing and when he talked it was as if his tongue was scattering pearls. It was a delight to listen to him. But then something happened which no one had foreseen. Listen! Among his fellow pupils were girls. Just like the boys, they came from noble families of various tribes. One day a beautiful little girl joined the group—a jewel such as one sees but seldom. She was as slender as a cypress tree. Her eyes, like those of a gazelle, could have pierced a thousand hearts with a single unexpected glance, yes, with one flicker of her eyelashes she could have slain a whole world.

To look at, she was like an Arabian moon, yet when it came to stealing hearts, she was a Persian page. Under the dark shadow of her hair, her face was a lamp, or rather a torch, with ravens weaving their wings around it. And who would have thought that

4

such overwhelming sweetness could flow from so small a mouth. Is it possible, then, to break whole armies with one small grain of sugar? She really did not need rouge; even the milk she drank turned into the color of roses on her lips and cheeks; and she was equipped with lustrous eyes and a mole on her cheek even when her mother brought her into the world.

The name of this miracle of creation was Layla. Does not 'Layl' mean 'night' in Arabic? And dark as the night was the color of her hair.

Whose heart would not have filled with longing at the sight of this girl? But young Qays felt even more. He was drowned in the ocean of love before he knew that there was such a thing. He had already given his heart to Layla before he understood what he was giving away... And Layla? She fared no better. A fire had been lit in both—and each reflected the other.

What could they have done against it? A bearer had come and filled their cups to the brim. They drank what he poured out for them. They were children and did not realize what they were drinking; no wonder they became drunk. He who is drunk for the first time, becomes deeply drunk indeed. And heavily falls he who has never had a fall before.

Together they had inhaled the scent of a flower, its name unknown, its magic great... As yet no one had noticed, so they went on drinking their wine and enjoying the sweet scent. They drank by day and dreamed by night, and the more they drank the deeper they became immersed in each other. Their eyes became blind and their ears deaf to the school and the world. They had found each other:

While all their friends were toiling at their books
These two were trying other ways of learning.
Reading love's grammar in each other's looks,
Glances to them were marks which they
                    were earning
Their minds were freed from spelliny by
                    love's spell,
They practiced, writing notes full of caress;
The others learned to count—while they
                    could tell
That nothing ever counts but tenderness.

III

HOW happy this first flowering of love for Qays and Layla! But can such happiness last? Was not a shadow already falling over their radiance—even if the children did not notice it? What did they know about the ways and the laws of this world? They did not count hours or days, until suddenly disaster struck.

Just as Joseph came out of his pit, so the sun, a golden orange, ascends every morning from the hem of the horizon like a precious toy in the sky; yet every evening, exhausted and worn out by the day's labor, it sinks back towards the west into the deep well. So Layla also shone forth in her morning. Every day she grew more beautiful. Not only Qays, also his companions at school became aware of it. Openly or secretly they began to stare at her; and if they caught only a glimpse of her chin, shaped like a lemon with little dimples, they felt like ripe pomegranates, full of juice, ready to burst with desire.

Was not Qays bound to notice? Certainly—and for the first time a bitter taste mingled with the sweet scent of his love. He was no longer alone with Layla. A small crack appeared in his blind happiness, he had a foreboding of what was to come; but it was too late.

While the lovers turned their backs on the world, drinking the wine of oblivion and enjoying their paradise, the eyes of the world turned towards them. Did the others understand what they saw? Could they decipher the secret code of signs and glances? How could they fail? But they understood in their own petty way, driven by curiosity, spurred by jealousy and spite and pleasure over other people's discomfiture! And how easy the lovers made it for their enemies to set their traps.

'What, you have not heard?' they sneered. And from mouth to mouth it was whispered, from ear to ear, from tent to tent.

When wagging tongues abused what was so fair,

7

Their eyes and lips could now no longer shield—
Caught by the gossip in the square—
The tender secret which each glance revealed.

Hard is the awakening for people so deeply intoxicated by their dreams. Now Layla and Qays began to notice the pointing fingers, to hear the reproaches, the derision, the whisperings behind their backs, to see strangers' eyes, watching, spying, following.

Suddenly they realized their blindness. Why had they never noticed the hunters and their weapons? Now they tried to mend the torn veil, to protect their naked love from the world, to hide their longing for each other, to tame their glances and to seal their lips.

They sought to be cautious and patient, but what use? Like the musk-deer, love, betrayed by its scent, cannot hide; like the sun, it penetrates clouds. Caution and patience are no chains for a lover already chained a thousand-fold by the tresses of his beloved. Qays' soul was a mirror for Layla's beauty—how could he remain silent about all he saw in it? How could he avert his glance from the fountain-head of his life?

He tried, but his heart was no longer at one with his reason. If reason asked him to avoid his love, his heart fell ill with longing for her. Away from her, Qays found no peace, yet searching her out was to imperil both.

8

Was there a way out? The youth could not see any, and his heart suddenly lost its balance, like a beast of burden, which stumbles and falls when the load on its back suddenly breaks loose. But those who never stumble nor fall, looked on and said, 'He is a majnun, a madman.'

Soon everyone knew and the more people saw and heard of him, the madder he appeared. But he did nothing to pacify those who reproached him. On the contrary, he walked among them, praising Layla's beauty—like a sleepwalker recalling a dream in the middle of the day. Who would do such a thing?

Disaster swiftly took its course. Too many hounds were chasing the stag, tongues hanging from their ravening mouths, barking and growling, panting and jeering.

It became too much for Layla's people. Was not the girl's honor also that of her family? More, that of her whole tribe? Was it right that this mad fellow, this Qays of the Banu Amir, should play around with her until her name became a laughing-stock?

From now on Layla's parents kept their daughter at home. They guarded her carefully and saw to it that Qays had no chance to meet her. They kept the new moon hidden from the fool; the way to the pastures was now blocked for the young gazelle. What could Layla do against it?

She had to hide the sadness of her heart. Only when

she was alone did she drop the curtain and shed lonely tears.

IV

THE separation from his beloved robbed the youth of his home, and if Layla wept secretly, he openly displayed his unhappiness for everyone to see.

He appeared now here, now there. He wandered about in the small alleys between the tents and in the bazaar where the merchants and artisans have their stalls. He walked aimlessly, driven only by his aching heart, without heeding the staring eyes; tears springing from under his eyelashes like wild mountain streams. All the time he sang melancholy songs such as lovers are wont to sing in their misery....

When he passed by, people around him shouted: 'Look, the Madman, Majnun, is coming.... Majnun!'

The reins had slipped from the rider's hand. His innermost being was revealed like the heart of a split fruit. He had not only lost his beloved, but also himself. Everyone saw in his face the reflection of the fire scorching his heart, saw the blood running from his wound. He was suffering because of his beloved, but she remained far away. The longer it lasted, the more Qays became Majnun. Burning like a candle, he did not sleep at night and, while he searched for a remedy to cure soul and body, both were filled with deadly pain. Each day, at dusk, the ghosts of his vain hopes chased him out into the desert, barefoot and bareheaded.

Then strange things began to happen. Majnun had been separated from Layla, yet his longing made him the slave of his imprisoned Mistress. A madman he became—but at the same time a poet, the harp of his love and of his pain.

At night, when everyone was asleep, he secretly stole to the tent of his beloved. Sometimes two or three friends who had suffered the torments of love like him, accompanied him on his wanderings, but mostly he was alone, reciting his poems. Swift as the north wind he flew along, kissed Layla's threshold like a shadow and returned before the new day dawned.

How hard it was to return! It seemed to take a year. On his way to her he ran fast, like water pouring into a trough. On the way back he crawled, as if he had to make his way through a hundred crevasses thick with thorn-bushes. If fate had allowed him happiness, he would never have returned home, where he now felt a stranger. His heart had suffered shipwreck, drifting helplessly in a boundless ocean; there seemed no end to the fury of the gale. He hardly listened to what people were saying; he no longer cared. Only when he heard Layla's name did he take notice. When they talked about other things, his ears and lips were sealed.

He walked around like a drunkard; weeping bitterly, he lurched, fell and jumped to his feet again. When Layla's tribe pitched their tents in the mountainous area of Najd, only there did he want to live. Once, when his strength failed him he gave a message for Layla to the east wind. These were his words:

'East wind, be gone early in the morning, caress her hair and whisper in her ear: "One who has sacrificed everything for you, lies in the dust on his way to you. He is seeking your breath in the blowing of the wind and tells his grief to the earth. Send him a breath of air as a sign that you are thinking of him."

'Oh my beloved, had I not given my soul to you, trembling with desire like the wind, it would have been better to lose it. I would not be worth the dust in which I am lying....Look, I am being consumed in the fire of my love, drowned in the tears of my unhappiness. Even the sun, which illumines the world, is singed by the heat of my sighs. Invisible candle of my soul, do not torture the night-moth fluttering around you. Your eyes have bewitched mine and sleep escapes them by day and by night.

'My longing for you is the consolation of my heart, its wound and its healing salve. If only you could send me the tiniest morsel of your sweet lips! The Evil Eye has suddenly separated me from you, my moon. My enemy has wrenched the juicy fruit from my hand and thrown me, so desperately thirsty, to the ground; now he points his fingers at me as I lie dying of my wounds. Yes, I am a victim of the world's Evil Eye, which has stolen what was my own. Who would not be afraid of it? People try to protect their children with blue amulets; even the sun, afraid of its darkness, wears a veil of pure sky-blue.

'But I was not protected by amulets, no veil covered my secret, no ruins offered a hiding-place for my treasure; that is why the world could rob me of it.'

V

ONCE more the young day donned his morning coat, woven from shimmering brocade. He adorned the ear of the sky with the precious golden ornament of the sun and the quicksilver of the stars melted in its red flames.

Majnun appeared, together with his friends, near the tent of his beloved. So far he had only come by night, wrapped in the cloak of darkness, but now he could bear it no longer. His patience was at an end; he had to see her, Layla, for whom his heart was crying out. The closer he came to his goal, the less certain were his steps; drunk with longing and confused by feverish hope, his lips trembled like the verses of the poem he was chanting.

Suddenly he stopped. In front of him he saw the tent—and what else? Seldom do dreams become so real. The curtain was withdrawn and in the entrance of the tent unveiled in the light of day, clearly visible against the dark interior, Layla was sitting; Layla, his moon.

Majnun sighed deeply. Now Layla saw him, and they recognized in the mirror of each other's face their own fear, their own pain and love. Neither stirred; only their eyes met, their voices caressed each other, softly exchanging plaintive sighs, which they were used to confide to the wind and to the night.

Layla was a lute, Majnun a viola.

All the radiance of this morning was Layla, yet a candle was burning in front of her, consuming itself with desire. She was the most beautiful garden and Majnun was a torch of longing. She planted the rose-bush; he watered it with his tears.

What shall I say about Layla? She was a fairy, not a human being. How shall I describe Majnun? He was a fairy's torch, alight from head to foot.

Layla was a jasmin-bush in spring, Majnun a meadow in autumn, where no jasmin was growing. Layla could bewitch with one glance from beneath her dark hair, Majnun was her slave and a dervish dancing before her. Layla held in her hand the glass of wine scented with musk. Majnun had not touched the wine, yet he was drunk with its sweet smell....

Only this encounter, brief and from afar was permitted to the lovers, then Majnun, afraid of guards and spies, ran away, lest the wheel of fate should turn even this fleeting happiness to disaster. He escaped from Layla in order to find her.

VI

MAJNUN'S secret sorties did not long remain hidden from Layla's people, who were incensed. By day and by night they guarded the whole area, to block the way against the disturber of the peace. The bridge between the two banks had fallen in; no sound reached the other side.

Still, Majnun continued to roam in the mountains of Najd. More and more often, and for ever lengthening spells, he left the dwelling-places and pastures of his tribe, wandering aimlessly through the desert, composing ghazals which he sang to himself. He was in rags and looked wilder each day. Overwhelmed by his melancholia, he did not listen to anyone or anything. Nothing that otherwise pleases or disturbs a man found an echo in his heart. His two or three companions had long since left him. From afar people pointed at him and said: 'There goes Majnun, the madman, the crazy one, who was once called Qays. He heaps shame and dishonor on himself and his people.'

There was not one among Majnun's people who did not feel ashamed of him. They had done all they could to avert disaster and help the youth in his trouble, but what good had that done in the end? Can one quench such a conflagration with good advice? And who of the counsellors had ever suffered such grief?

Still, it could not go on like this. Not only the lover's sanity, but the reputation of his family, of the whole tribe was at stake. Was not Qays' father the leader of the Amir?

He was, and no one was so shaken by the disaster which his son caused and suffered. Yet even he could not change the course of fate. He was an old man, growing rapidly older under the strain.

When Majnun's state, far from improving, deteriorated even further, his father, the Sayyid, one day assembled all the counsellors and elders in his tent. He asked everyone and each told what he knew. The story was long and sad, and when the old man had heard it from beginning to end, his head sank lower and his heart grew heavier. What could be done? After he had considered carefully what he had heard, he spoke: 'My son has lost his heart to this girl; if he could only win her, he would find himself again. His senses are confused, because for him this jewel is the eye of the world. As it is hidden from him, he lives in darkness, a blind man. We must find his pearl. If we brush the dust from the budding rose, it will break into bloom.'

Then the Sayyid asked all the elders, one after the other, to give their opinion—and behold, they all agreed! Trying to win for the sleepwalker his moon, a delegation was to be sent to Layla's tribe.

No sooner said than done, and the old Sayyid led the dignitaries on their way. His sadness gone, he was full of confidence that he could untie the knot in his son's life-thread.

There was no feud between the two tribes, so, when the visitors arrived, they were received by Layla's people high and humble with great friendliness, feasted and treated with great deference. Only then did the hosts turn to the Sayyid, asking politely what he desired.

'Tell us why you have come,' they said. 'If you are in need of help, it will be granted. We count it an honor to assist you.'

'These young people, on whose behalf I am approaching you, will strengthen the ties between us,' responded the Sayyid of the Amiri tribe.

Then he looked at Layla's father, who was accompanied by the dignitaries of his tribe, and said to him:

'May your daughter and my son enhance each other's lives! Behold, I have come to establish a close link between us. I ask for your child's hand on behalf of

my own. Both have grown up in the same desert. My
son is thirsting to drink from your fountain, and such
pure drink will restore him, body and soul....Nor
have I any cause to be ashamed of my request. There
is, as you know, no man among us whose standing is
higher than mine. I have many followers and great
riches, I can be a valuable friend or a formidable
enemy. Whatever you demand as a dowry shall be
yours. I have come as a buyer, and you, if you are
wise, will state your price and sell. Take note, there is
a chance of great gain for you today; tomorrow it may
be too late. Do not forget how often prices fall
suddenly in the bazaar!'

Thus spoke the Sayyid. Anxiety for his son
sharpened his tongue. But Layla's father was a proud,
hard man. After the Amiri had finished, this was his
reply:

'What you say is your own affair, but you cannot
change fate or the course of the world by words. You
speak well and your words are full of sap, but do you
really think that enough to lure me into the fire? You
have shown me the attractive cover, but what lies
hidden underneath, causing my enemies greatly to
rejoice, you have not mentioned. Your son is a stately
youth and, seen from afar, would be welcome
anywhere. But don't we all know better than that?
Who has not heard more than enough about him and
his foolishness? Who is not aware of his madness? He
is mad, and a madman is no son-in-law for us.

Therefore you had better pray first that he be cured; afterwards you may mention marriage again, but until then there can be no question of it. Nobody would buy a faulty jewel to be set with flawless ones. And there is something else! You know only too well how keen-eyed and sharp-tongued Arabs are. What would they say, and how would they jeer, if I did what you suggest. Forget, therefore, what you have said!'

This was a bitter pill for Majnun's father to swallow, but what could he say? He remained silent, and so did his companions. All they could do was to depart. It was a sad homecoming for them, who had set out so certain of success.

VII

WHEN Majnun's father and his friends had failed to obtain Layla's hand, they tried once more to cure the youth by warnings and good advice. 'Why,' so they said, 'do you worship only this girl Layla? Look around among the girls of your own tribe. You will find so many with lips like hyacinths, sweet-scented and dressed in Egyptian linen; beauties who are perhaps even more attractive than she who has stolen your heart. You are free to choose from among a hundred maidens, each of them lovelier than the new spring. Find a companion who will be a comfort to you instead of torturing your heart, a girl like milk and honey, worthy of you. Let the foreigner go!'

Thus his friends talked; their intentions were good, but what did they know about the fire burning in Majnun's soul? Their words nursed the conflagration like thorn-bushes; prickly at first, they soon began to burn and increased the flame which they were meant to smother.

No; Majnun was now doubly in despair about the answer of Layla's father and the warnings of his own people. Nothing could sweeten the bitterness which transformed his world into darkest night. Expelled from the land of happiness, he was now a stranger in either world. He beat his head with his fists and rent his garment from top to bottom. Even a corpse has at least a shroud, but then a corpse is at home in his grave—Majnun had no home anywhere.

He left his father and his relatives and ran away, paying no attention to roads and directions. He called out: 'There is no power and no might except with Allah.' And, truly, God alone knows how the unhappy youth overcame his desire to kill himself, for everything that binds human beings had fallen away from him.

He no longer knew what was good and what was evil, and could not distinguish the one from the other. Through every tent rang out his cry, 'Layla... Layla!'

His hair fell unkempt about his face, his eyes stared; yet he saw nothing of his fellow men, nor heard their reproaches.

The crowd who watched and followed him was growing all the time. They were greatly upset by his behavior, but when he began to talk in verse and sing about his love; when he addressed the star of his longing; when the fire in his heart reached the tip of his tongue and sadness resounded from his lips, the mood of his listeners changed. They stood surprised and deeply moved, and soon there was no one who did not shed tears about the minstrel and his fate.

Majnun, however, noticed neither reproach nor sympathy. He was not even aware of the people around him. It was as if his name had been torn out of the Book of Life, and he had fallen into nothingness; as if he were no longer one of the living, and not yet one of the dead. A stone had dropped on his heart; he was like a burnt-out candle, or a maimed bird that has lost its mate and flutters helplessly in the dust. In the end strength left his body. He fell to his knees as if at prayer, and cried until consciousness returned and he felt pain flowing over his lips like a dark stream:

'Oh, who can cure my sickness? An outcast I have become. Family and home, where are they? No path leads back to them and none to my beloved. Broken are my name, my reputation, like glass smashed on a rock; broken is the drum which once spread the good news, and my ears now hear only the drumbeat of separation.

'Huntress, beautiful one, whose victim I am— limping, a willing target for your arrows. I follow obediently my beloved, who owns my soul. If she says "Get drunk," that is what I shall do. If she orders me to be mad, that is what I shall be. To tame a madman like me, fate has no chains; crushed as I am, what hope is there that I could ever be revived? Heaven grant that a rockfall may crush and bury me, or that lightning may strike me, burning down the house with all its furnishings! Is there no one who will throw me into the crocodile-jaws of death, no one who will free me from myself, and the world from my shame? Misbegotten creature, madman, demon of my family!

'Yes, I am a thorn in the flesh of my people, and even my name brings shame upon my friends. Anyone may shed my blood; I am outlawed, and who kills me is not guilty of murder.

'Goodbye to you, companions of past feastings. I salute you. Farewell! Look, the wine is spilled, the glass has slipped from my hands and broken. Of my happiness only the shards are left, with sharp edges which cause deep anguish. But when you come, do not be afraid of cutting your feet. The flood of my tears has swept away the shards—far, far, away.'

Did Majnun notice the people who surrounded him

silently, staring and listening? So it seemed, for he turned and spoke to them:

'What do you know, who have no notion of my grief? Away with you, make room! Do not look for me; I am not where you believe me to be. I am lost, even to myself! One does not address people like me! You torture and oppress me. How much longer? Leave me alone with my unhappiness. No need to chase me from your tents, I shall go freely—I am going!'

But Majnun no longer had the strength to flee. He fell on his knees in the dust. Again and again, in deep desperation, his heart went out to Layla, who was so far away, and implored her to help him.

'I have fallen; what shall I do? Oh, my beloved, come and take my hand. I can endure it no longer, I am yours, more use to you alive than dead. Be generous and send a greeting, send a message to revive me. You are imprisoned, I know. But why imprison you? I am the madman, I should be fettered. Bind me to you, wind again your tresses round my neck; they are torn, yet I remain your slave. Do something; help me! This is a cruel game. End it! Lift your foot that I may kiss it.... Things cannot remain as they are. It is not right to sit in the corner, arms folded, doing nothing. Take pity on me. A rested man has no feeling for one who is exhausted. A rich man, his hunger stilled, who invites a beggar to his table, knows nothing about starvation. Yet he may eat a few morsels to honor his guest. Aren't we both human beings, you as well as

I, even if you are a blossoming beech tree while I am a dry thorn-bush?

'Peace of my soul, where are you? Why do you rob me of my life? Other than my love, what is the sin of my heart, this heart which asks for your forgiveness? Of a thousand nights give me only one. Look, everything else I have gambled away and lost.

'Do not say "No". If you are angry with me, quench the fire of your wrath with the water of my tears. I am a star, my new moon, driven to distraction by my longing to see you. My only companion is my shadow, and even with him I do not dare to talk, fearing lest he might become a rival. If only your shadow had stayed with me, but even that you have taken away, and my heart and soul with it. What did I receive in return? What is left to me? Hope? A thirsty child may well, in a dream, see a hand offering a golden cup, but when he wakes, what remains? All that he can do is suck his fingers to quench his thirst. What does it matter! Nothing can ever extinguish the love for you in my heart. It is a riddle without a solution, a code which none can decipher. It entered my body with my mother's milk—to leave it only together with my soul, of that I am sure.'

Here Majnun fell silent. His voice failed and, unconscious, he fell forward, his face in the dust. All who had listened to him and saw him lying there, felt sad. Gently they lifted the unhappy youth and carried him home to his father's tent.

Love, if not true, is but a plaything of the senses, fading like youth. Time perishes, not true love. All may be imagination and delusion, but not love. The charcoal brazier on which it burns is eternity itself, without beginning or end.

Majnun won fame as a lover, for he carried love's burden as long as he lived. Love was the flower's scent and the breath of the wind. Even now, when the rose has faded, a drop of the rose-water endures and will last for ever, giving pleasure to you, reader, and to Nizami.

VIII

THE further away his moon, Layla, shone in the sky, the higher Majnun waved the banner of his love! As his mad passion grew day by day, so his repute declined among his friends.

But as yet his family and, above all, his father, had not given up hope that his dark night might end and a new morning dawn. Once more they took counsel, and, having talked for a long time without result, their thoughts finally converged on the Kaaba, God's sanctuary in Mecca, visited every year by thousands and thousands of faithful pilgrims from near and far.

'Well,' they said, 'could it not happen after all that the Almighty One would come to our aid, that the door for which we have no key would suddenly open? Is not the Kaaba the Altar of heaven and earth, where the whole world prays for God's blessing and help. Why not we?'

Majnun's father, the old Sayyid, agreed. He prepared everything he thought necessary, and when the month of pilgrimage, the twelfth and last of the year, had come, he left with a small caravan for the Holy City. He had chosen his best camels for the journey; and for Majnun, the apple of his eye, he had secured a litter, which carried the lovesick youth as gently as a moon's cradle.

They reached Mecca safely. As he had done on the way, the leader of the tribe showered alms on the crowd, like a dust-storm, which carries gold coins instead of sand. But a storm raged also in his breast and the nearer they came to their goal, the more excited he became. Devoured by hope and impatience he could hardly wait for the moment when he would be able to entrust his sorrow-child to the grace of the Almighty.

At last the time had come; father and son stood in the shadow and protection of the Holiest of Holies. Gently the Sayyid took the youth by the hand and said to him:

'Here, my dearest son, every play comes to its end. Try to find relief from your sufferings. Here, in front of this temple and its Master, you must pray to be freed from your sorrow. Listen; this should be your prayer: "Save me, my God, from this vain ecstasy. Have pity on me; grant me refuge; take my madness away and lead me back to the path of righteousness. I am love's unhappy victim! Help me! Free me from the evil of my love." Recite this prayer, my son.'

When Majnun heard his father speaking he wept, then began to laugh. Suddenly, a strange thing happened. He darted forward like the head of a coiled snake, stretched out his hands towards the door of the temple, hammered against it, and shouted:

'Yes, it is I, who knocks at this door today! I have sold my life for love's sake! Yes, it is I; may I always be love's slave! They tell me: abandon love, that is the path to recovery—but I can gain strength only through love. If love dies, so shall I. My nature is love's pupil; be my fate nothing, if not love, and woe to the heart incapable of passion. I ask thee, my God, I beseech thee, in all the godliness of thy divine nature and all the perfection of thy kingdom: let my love grow stronger, let it endure, even if I perish. Let me drink from this well, let my eye never miss its light. If I am drunk with the wine of love, let me drink even more deeply.

'They tell me: "Crush the desire for Layla in your heart!" But I implore thee, oh my God, let it grow even stronger. Take what is left of my life and add it to Layla's. Let me never demand from her as much as a single hair, even if my pain reduces me to the width of one! Let her punish and castigate me: her wine alone shall fill my cup, and my name shall never appear without her seal. My life shall be sacrificed for her beauty, my blood shall be spilled freely for her, and though I burn for her painfully, like a candle, none of my days shall ever be free of this pain. Let me love, oh my God, love for love's sake, and make my love a hundred times as great as it was and is!'

Such was Majnun's prayer to the Almighty. His father listened silently. What could he say? He knew now that he could not loosen the fetters binding this heart, could not find a cure for its ills. There was nothing to do but to leave Mecca and start on the trek home, where they were awaited impatiently in sorrow and fear. When they arrived, the whole family surrounded the Sayyid: 'How was it?' they clamored. 'Tell us! Has Allah helped? Is he saved ?'

But the old man's eyes looked tired and sad. 'I have tried,' he said; 'I have told him how to ask God for relief from this plague, this Layla. But he clung to his own ideas. What did he do? He cursed himself and blessed Layla.'

IX

THE pilgrimage to Mecca and the old Sayyid's vain attempt to heal his son's madness was talked about everywhere. Soon there was no tent whose inhabitants did not know about it. The story of Majnun's love was on everybody's lips. Some reproached him and jeered, others pitied and tried to defend him. Many spread evil rumors; a few even spoke well of him—sometimes.

Bedouin gossip came also to Layla's ears, but what could she do about it? She remained silent, in secret grief. The members of her tribe, however, angry and bitter, sent mounted emissaries to the caliph's prefect and laid a complaint against the youth.

'This madman,' the two delegates said, 'imperils by his behavior, the honor of our tribe. Day after day he trails around the countryside, his hair dishevelled and a bunch of hooligans running after him like a pack of hounds loosed from their chains. Now he dances, now he kisses the soil. All the time he composes and recites his ghazals. And as, unfortunately, his verses are good and his voice pleasant, people learn these songs by heart. That is bad both for you and for us, because whatever this impertinent fellow composes tears the veils of custom and decency a hundred-fold. Through him Layla is branded with a hot iron, and if this perilous wind continues to blow it will extinguish the lamp. Order, therefore, his punishment, so that Layla, our moon, may henceforth be safe from this plague.'

The caliph's prefect, having listened to their speech, drew his sword out of its sheath, showed it to the two

emissaries, and replied: 'Give your answer with this!'
By chance a man from the tribe of Amir happened to
overhear. What did he do? He went to the Sayyid and
reported:

'So far nothing untoward has happened,' he said, 'but
I warn you: this prefect is out for blood; he is a raging
torrent and a blazing fire. Seeing that Majnun does
not know the danger threatening him, I am afraid
that by the time he realizes it, it may be too late. We
must warn him of this open well, lest he fall into it.'

That is how the informant spoke and his words stung
the father's wounded heart like salt. He feared for his
son's life; but however anxiously they searched for
him, he was not to be found. In the end all the men
sent out to trace him, came back discouraged. 'Who
knows,' they said, 'perhaps his fate has already
overtaken him? Perhaps wild animals have torn him
to pieces, or even worse has happened to him.'

Whereupon the youth's kinsmen and companions
raised wailings and lamentations as if they were
mourning the dead.

But Majnun was not dead. As before, he had gone to
a hiding-place in the wilderness. There he was living
alone, a hidden treasure; he neither saw nor heard
what was happening in the world. In that world, were
they not all hunters and hunted? Did that still
concern him? Had he not turned his back on it? Had
he not troubles enough of his own? He did not want

the pity of his fellow men. He suffered because he could not find the treasure for which he was searching; yet his grief provided him with a free passage, liberating him from the fetters of selfishness.

Now let us see what happened then. After a time, chance brought a Bedouin from the Saad tribe walking along the same path. When he saw the lonely figure crouching in solitude, he at first suspected a mirage—a *fata Morgana;* who else would keep his own shadow company in such a place?

But when he heard a soft moaning, he went nearer and asked: 'Who are you? What are you doing here? How can I help you?'

However often he repeated his questions he received no answer. In the end his patience became exhausted; he continued on his way, but when he arrived home he told his family about the strange encounter.

'On my way through a mountain gorge I met a creature writhing on the stones like a snake, like a madman in pain, like a lonely demon; his body was so wasted that every bone was visible.'

When Majnun's father heard about it he set out at once to bring home his lost son from the wilderness. He reached the hiding-place and found Majnun as the Bedouin had described him: now talking to himself in verse, now moaning and sighing. He wept, stood up and collapsed again, he crawled and

31

stumbled, a living image of his own fate. He swooned and was hardly conscious, so that at first he did not recognize his own father. But then, when the Sayyid addressed and comforted him, the firmness of his voice brought Majnun back to himself. He collapsed at the old man's feet like a shadow, and implored him in regret and despair:

'Crown of my head and haven of my soul, forgive me, forgive. Do not ask how I am, because you can see that I am weak. I wish you had been spared the pain of finding me in this state. Now you have come, my face turns black with shame! Forgive me; you know only too well how things are with me, but you also know that it is not ourselves who hold fate's thread in our hands.'

X

THE father tore the turban from his head and threw it to the ground. The day became as dark in his eyes as the night and he raised a plaintive song like a bird at dusk.

But then he summoned his courage and spoke:

'Rose petal, torn and crumpled! Love's fool, uncontrolled, immature, your heart burned! What evil eye has cast a spell over your beauty? Whose curse has blighted you? For whose blood must you do penance? Whose thorn has torn the hem of your robe? What has pushed you into this abyss?

'True, you are young, and youth has led many into confusion before—but not so deeply. Is your heart still not satiated with pain? Have you still not born enough abuse and reproach? Will there be no resurrection for you on earth? Enough! You are destroying yourself with your passion— and me and my honor as well. If one day you hope to marry, such lack of self-control is a great fault. Even if we do not like to show our weakness to the world, we should have friends, genuine and true like mirrors, clearly revealing our faults so that we can face and cure them. Let me be your mirror. Free your heart from this illness. Do not try any longer to forge a cold iron.'

Sadness in his voice, the old man continued:

'Perhaps you are not patient enough. You are persistent only in keeping away from me, your friend. You hardly look at me. But he who flees and keeps aloof, remains alone with the longing of his heart. Do you not know that? You try to become drunk without wine, you worship desire for its own sake. You have fled and left the harvest to the wind, you have abandoned me to the gloating satisfaction of my enemies. Regain your senses before it is too late. Do not forget: while you are playing the harp of your love, I am mourning for you, and when you are rending your garments asunder you are tearing my soul. When your heart burns, you also burn mine. Do not despair. Some little thing, useless as it may appear to you, can bring salvation. Despair may lead to hope just as night leads to dawn, if only you have faith. Look for the company of gay people, do not flee from happiness. Bliss can undo all knots; it is the turquoise in the seal of God. It will come to you, only you must have patience. Let your happiness grow slowly. Even the mighty sea consists of single drops; even the mountain, cloud-high, of tiny grains of earth. And have you not all the time in the world? With patience, you can search at ease for the precious stone. Be prudent! The dumb fall behind, like the worm without feet, but the clever fox can overcome the stronger wolf. Why do you give your heart to a rose? She blossoms without you, while you remain in the mud; she has a heart of stone—indeed, your heart is being stoned! Why?

'They who talk to you about Layla seek your shame and disgrace. They offer you parsley which is poison to a man stung by a scorpion. You must see that, my son. Give up!

'You are dearer to me than life itself. Come home and stay with us. Here in the mountains only tears await you; you will find nothing but stones on this path, and deep wells in which you will drown. Do not argue! Even the prefect is out to destroy you, and if you play with madness you are forging an iron chain for yourself.... Watch the sword, my child, drawn to smite you and take care of your life, while there is time. Make new friends, be gay, and laugh at the discomfort of your enemies!'

XI

WHEN the old Sayyid had thus poured out all the hopes and sorrows stored up in his heart, Majnun could remain silent no longer, and this was his reply:

'You, whose Majesty equals that of Heaven itself, King of all our dwelling-places, inhabited or deserted, pride and glory of all Arabs, I kneel before you. I have received my life from you, may you never lose your own, and may I never lose you. Your words are scorching me—yet what can I do? I, the man with the blackened face, have not chosen the way, I have been cast on to it. I am manacled, and my fetters, as you say, are made of iron. But it was not I who forged them; it was my fate, my Kismet, that decided. I cannot loosen them; I cannot throw off my burden. Not of its own will does the shadow fall into the depth of the well, not by its own power does the moon rise in the sky to its zenith. Wherever you look, from ant to elephant, you will find no object or creature, which is not ruled by fate.

'Who, therefore, could remove the load of stone from my heart? Who could wash away the disaster which is crushing me, which I have not chosen. I am carrying the burden which has been put on my shoulders, and cannot throw it off. You keep asking me, "Why do you never laugh?" But tears rather than laughter become the sufferer. If I were to laugh, it would be as if lightning and thunder were laughing as they broke the clouds; the fire burning inside me would scorch my lips, and I would perish in the furnace of my mirth....'

Here Majnun interrupted himself and told this story to the Sayyid:

THE FABLE OF THE PARTRIDGE AND THE ANT

'There was once a partridge, which, when hunting, espied an ant, and seized in its beak one of the ant's legs. It was just about to swallow it when the ant laughed and shouted: "Partridge, to laugh as I do, that's one thing you are not capable of!"

'The partridge was greatly upset. It did not stop to think; it just opened its beak to laugh heartily and said: "Really, it is my turn to laugh, and not yours." But by that time the ant had escaped from the re-opened prison, and the silly partridge was left alone in the field.

'Man, if he laughs at the wrong time, will fare no better; he will regret with tears that he laughed too soon.'

XII

'I ALSO,' Majnun continued, 'have no reason to laugh. Even the old donkey does not throw down its burden before death takes it away. Why then should it fear death? You warned me, father; but what lover goes in fear of the sword? A man in love does not tremble for his life. He who searches for his beloved is not afraid of the world. Where is this sword? Let it smite me, as the cloud has swallowed my moon. My soul has fallen into the fire, and even if it hurts to lie there, no matter; it was good to fall.

'Leave my soul alone. It is destroyed, it is lost; what do you want from it?'

When the old man heard this, he shed bitter tears and, smarting with pain, took his disturbed son home. There the family nursed him, comforting him as best they could. They also called on his former friends, and entrusted the child of sorrow to their care.

But for Majnun they were all strangers. Life at home was one prolonged torture to him, and all who saw him felt tears come into their eyes. How could they help such a heart? For two or three days Majnun bore the strain, then he tore down the curtain which his friends had put up to protect him and escaped once more into the desert of Najd. Like a drunken lion he

roamed restlessly about in this desolate country of
sand and rocks. His feet became as hard as iron, the
palms of his hands like stone. He wandered through
the mountains chanting his ghazals. But how strange!
Even if Majnun was mad, his verses were not. Even if
people heaped abuse and shame on him, they could
find no fault in his verses.

Many came from near and far to hear the minstrel in
his mountain retreat. Listening eagerly and loving
what they heard, they wrote down his poems and
took them away to the farthest horizons. Some
became lovers themselves.

XIII

IN the meantime Layla had grown daily more
beautiful. The promise of the bud had been kept
by the blossom. Half an enticing glance from her eyes
would have been enough to conquer a hundred kings;
she could have plundered Arab or Turk, had she
wanted.

Nobody could escape such a huntress. With her
gazelle's eyes she caught her victims and tied them
with the rope of her tresses. Even a lion would have
bent his neck gracefully under such a yoke.

A flower was Layla's face; anyone who looked at her,
fell hungry for the honey of her lips, and turned

beggar for her kisses; but her eyelashes refused to give alms, and said, 'May God grant you what you desire, I shall give nothing.'

Those who had been caught by the noose of her locks were chased away by the darts of her eyelashes. Her body was like a cypress tree on which the pheasant of her face was sitting in majesty. Hundreds of lost hearts had already fallen into the well of her dimples, but our beauty took pity on those who had lost their footing and threw them her tresses as a rope to the rescue. So powerful was the spell of Layla's beauty.

Yet this enchantress could not help herself. Seen from outside she seemed to blossom; inside she shed tears of blood. Secretly she was looking for Majnun from morning till night; and at midnight, when nobody could hear, her sighs were calling him. Her laughter was born of tears, like the light of a candle, and out of all they saw, her eyes formed the image of her beloved.

Like Majnun, ever since their separation, she also burned in the fire of longing; but her flames were hidden and no smoke rose from them. Layla, too, had her 'mirror of pain' like the one which the doctor holds in front of a dying man's mouth to see whether a breath of life still clouds the glass; but Layla's mirror was her own soul which in her loneliness she questioned about her beloved. With whom else could she talk about the thoughts which filled her heart? At night she told the secret to her shadow. She lived between the water of her tears and the fire of her love, as if she were a Peri, a fairy, hovering between fire and water.

Though devoured by sorrow, Layla would not have told her grief for anything in the world. Sometimes, when no one was awake, the fountains of the moon made her step outside. There she stood, her eyes fixed on the path, waiting—for whom? Did she hope that a messenger might pass by or even call upon her? But only the wind blowing from the mountains of Najd brought a breath of faith from a lonely man, or drove a cloud across, whose rain was, for Layla, a greeting from afar.

Yet her lover's voice reached her. Was he not a poet? No tent curtain was woven so closely as to keep out his poems. Every child from the bazaar was singing his verses; every passer-by was humming one of his love-songs, bringing Layla a message from her beloved, whether he knew it or not.

Now Layla was not only a picture of gracefulness, but also full of wisdom and well versed in poetry. She herself, a pearl unpierced, pierced the pearls of words, threading them together in brilliant chains of poems. Secretly she collected Majnun's songs as they came to her ears, committed them to memory and then composed her answers.

These she wrote down on little scraps of paper, heading them with the words: 'Jasmin sends this message to the cypress tree.' Then, when no one was looking, she entrusted them to the wind.

It happened often that someone found one of these little papers, and guessed the hidden meaning, realizing for whom they were intended. Sometimes he would go to Majnun hoping to hear, as a reward, some of the poems which had become so popular.

And, true enough, there was no veil which could hide his beloved from Majnun. He answered at once, in verse, and whoever received the message saw to it that Layla should hear it at once.

Thus many a melody passed to and fro between the two nightingales, drunk with their passion. Those who heard them listened in delight, and so similar were the two voices that they sounded like a single chant. Born of pain and longing, their song had the power to break the unhappiness of the world.

XIV

I N the garden, blossoms were smiling from all the trees. This morning the earth had hoisted a twin-colored banner of red tulips and yellow roses; and the tulips threw vermilion-red petals, with black sun-spots, over the emerald-green carpet of the lawn, still glistening with pearls of dew.

As if playing, the violets hid from each other on their

long, curved stems; the rosebud girded itself and pointed thorny lances, ready for battle, while the water-lily, as if pausing in the fight, was resting her shield flat on the mirror-like surface of the pond. The hyacinth had opened wide her cups, the box tree was combing its hair, the blossoms of the pomegranate tree were longing for their own fruit, the narcissus glowing fiercely suddenly woke from a bad dream frightened like a feverish patient.

The sun had opened the veins of the Judas tree, full of blood, like wine; the wild rose was washing her leaves in the jasmin's silver fountain, and the iris wielded her sword fiercely.

In every plane tree the ringdoves cooed their love-stories, and on the topmost branch the nightingale was sitting, sighing like Majnun; while below, the rose lifted her head out of her calyx towards the bird, like Layla.

On one such happy day, when the roses were in full bloom, Layla came with some friends into the garden, to enjoy themselves among the beautiful flowers like the maidens in the garden of paradise.

Did she intend to rest in the red shadow of the roses? Or did she want to enrich the green of the grass with her own shadow, and lift her cup together with narcissus and tulip? Did she come as a victor to demand tribute from the kingdom of these gardens in all their splendor?

Oh no! None of that was in her mind. She had come to lament, like those burned by the flame of love. She wanted to talk to the nightingale, drunk with passion; tell her secret, describe her sufferings; perhaps Zephir, breathing through the rose-gardens, would bring a sign from afar, from the beloved.

Layla was trying to find comfort in the garden; she looked at it as an ornament framing the image of the beloved; perhaps it could show her the way to that other garden, the garden of paradise?

But of that the friends who accompanied Layla, knew nothing. For a while the girls walked among the roses, and wherever they passed, with their figures like cypress trees and their tulip-like faces, the flowers, as if in rivalry, blossomed twice as beautifully.

While the maidens, in merriment and laughter, rested in a secluded corner of the garden, Layla walked on unnoticed and sat down far from them, under a shady tree. There she could air her lament, as her heart desired, like a nightingale in spring.

'O my faithful one,' she sighed, 'are you not made for me, and I for you? Noble youth with the passionate heart, how ice-cold is the breath of separation! If only you would now walk through the gate of this garden, to heal my wounded heart. If only you could sit next to me, looking into my eyes, fulfilling my deepest desire, you my elm, and I your cypress... But who knows, perhaps you have already suffered so much for my sake that you can no longer enjoy my love, nor the beauty of the garden....'

While Layla was thus dreaming of her beloved, suddenly a loud voice reached her ear. Someone was passing the garden, singing to himself. The voice was that of a stranger, but the lines were well known to her; she recognized Majnun's verses at once:

Majnun is torn by grief and suffering,
Yet Layla's garden blooms as if in spring.
How can his Love live joyfully, at rest
And smile, while arrows pierce him, at a jest?

When Layla heard this melancholy strain she broke into tears and wept so bitterly that it would have softened a stone. She had no idea that anyone was watching, but one of the girls had noticed her absence. Inquisitive, as girls are, she had followed behind, had heard the stranger's song and had seen the tears in Layla's eyes. Both surprised and frightened her.

Returning home from the garden, she went secretly to Layla's mother and told her what she had observed. The mother lost her head like a bird caught in a trap. What was she to do? She suffered with her daughter; yet however hard she tried, she could not think of a remedy.

'I must not allow Layla to do what her heart urges,'

44

she told herself, 'because that youth is a madman; he will infect her with his own insanity. But if I urge her to be patient she, unable to bear it, may break down completely—and I with her.'

So the daughter's suffering became a torment for the mother. Layla did not realize it; she did not reveal her secret and so her mother, too, remained silent.

XV

O N the day of her visit to the garden, where so much else happened, Layla also saw by chance a youth from the tribe of Asad passing by on his travels. His name, Ibn Salam, was of good repute among the Arabs. He was a young nobleman; when people saw him, they pointed him out, not in reproach, but as one is wont to single out a person of high renown. He had many kinsmen and belonged to a great tribe; nobody would close his ears to Ibn Salam's greetings.

Wherever he appeared, people said: 'Look, here comes the good luck of Ibn Salam...,' and so, 'Good Luck,' 'Bakht,' had become his nickname. A true gentleman, he was strong and generous. One glance at the moon, just fourteen days old, and he decided to conquer this shining light. Unable to forget her, he thought of her ceaselessly on his journey home—and even more afterwards. Did he not have great riches?

Used as he was to act, he went to work, swift as the wind. One point only he did not consider—whether his wind would be welcomed by the shining light, whether the moon would tolerate his embrace....

Otherwise, this resourceful man thought of everything. According to custom, he at once sent a confidant to Layla's parents, to ask for the fairy-girl's hand in marriage. This man was briefed to propose, submissively like a beggar, in well calculated humility, but at the same time to offer presents like a king and to squander gold as if it were sand.

And that is how it went. Who could have refused such a match-maker ? But, however favorably father and mother listened to him, it seemed too early to give their final consent. Why decide today, when there was a tomorrow? Was it not more prudent to wait, since there was a chance of waiting?

They did not refuse, they just bade him tarry. Generously they spread the ointment of hope and said:

'What you are asking for may well be granted; only have a little patience. Look! This spring flower is not very strong—somewhat pale she is, somewhat too delicate. Allow her first to gain strength, then we shall agree with pleasure to the union. May this soon happen, God willing— inshallah. A few days more, a few less, what does it matter? It will not be long before this rosebud blossoms and the thorn-bush has been cleared from the garden gate.'

That was the parents' answer; and Ibn Salam had to be content and wait.

XVI

LET us see what was happening to Majnun in the meantime. The gorge in which he had chosen to live belonged to an area ruled by a Bedouin prince called Nawfal. Because of his bravery in battle he was called 'Destroyer of Armies', but though iron-hard in front of the enemy, he was as soft as wax in kindness towards his friends. A lion in war, he was a gazelle in love, and widely renowned in the country for both.

One day this chieftain, Nawfal, rode out to hunt with some of his companions. The country became wilder and more and more desolate, but the hunters had eyes only for their prey, and when some of the light-legged antelopes and wild donkeys tried to escape into their hiding-places in the mountains, Nawfal and his friends followed swiftly.

But suddenly the mighty warrior reined in his horse. What was wrong? Only a few steps ahead, in the semi-darkness at the entrance to a cave, two or three of the animals were huddled together, their flanks trembling—yet the hunter suddenly dropped his bow with the arrow on its drawn string. Surprised, he stared towards the grotto, where he noticed, behind an antelope's back, a living being such as he had never encountered before.

The creature was crouching against the side of the rock, naked, wasted, arms and legs severely scratched by thorns, long strands of hair falling over the shoulders and the hollow cheeks. Was it an animal or a human being, a savage or one of the dead—maybe a demon? But the creature was weeping, so all fear vanished, giving way to pity. The noble hunter turned in the saddle towards his men and asked: 'Does anyone know who this unhappy creature is?'

'Certainly, we have heard of him,' replied several voices. Then one man, who seemed to know more about it, stepped forward and said:

'The youth over there has become what he is through his love for a woman. He is a melancholic, a madman, who has left the company of men and now lives here in the desert. Day and night he composes poems for his beloved. If a gust of wind sweeps by, or a cloud sails past in the sky, he believes them to be greetings from her and he thinks he can inhale her scent. He recites his poems, hoping that the wind or a cloud will carry them along to his beloved.'

'How can he live here alone?' asked Nawfal.

'Oh, people come to visit him,' said the man, 'some even undertake long voyages and suffer great hardship because they want to see him. They carry food and drink to him and sometimes visitors even offer him wine. But he eats and drinks very little, and if he is persuaded to sip the wine, he does so remembering his beloved. He thinks and acts only for her!'

Nawfal listened attentively and his sympathy for Majnun grew with every word. The hunt was forgotten.

'In truth,' he exclaimed, 'would it not be a manly deed, an act truly worthy of me, to help this confused, wayward fellow win his heart's ardent desire?'

With these words he jumped from his mount—a thoroughbred ambling on reed-like fetlocks—and ordered a tent to be erected, a dining table prepared and the youth brought in as his guest.

Everything was arranged as he demanded, and how amiable, how heart-stirring a host Nawfal could be! But for the first time all his artful pains seemed to be in vain. However much he urged and insisted, the recluse from the mountains would not touch any of the tempting dishes offered to him; not one bite, not one sip. And the merrier the chieftain became, the more he talked and joked, the less the poet seemed to listen, the more deaf and blind he seemed to become.

What was to be done? In the end, Nawfal, who had given up all hope, mentioned casually the name which his men had revealed to him: Layla!

And behold, as if touched by a magic wand, the youth lifted his head; for the first time his eyes betrayed his feelings, and he repeated smilingly 'Layla..., nothing but Layla.'

Then he helped himself, ate a morsel, took a sip. Nawfal understood. He talked about nothing but Layla; he praised her beauty, extolled her virtue, glorified her appearance, her character.

And Majnun responded. When the Bedouin chieftain, with his clever tongue, wove garlands of flowers, the lover added the shimmering pearls of his poems; although invented the moment they were sung, they were sweet and glowing like honey and fire. Nawfal listened in surprise and admiration. The man sitting in front of him was perhaps a savage, a fool—but there was no doubt that he was a poet, and among poets a master whose equal was not to be found in the whole of Arabia.

Quietly Nawfal made up his mind to rebuild with wary hands, the ruin of this heart stone by stone. Aloud he said:

'You are like the butterfly, my friend, which flutters around in the darkness, searching for the light. Take care that you do not become a candle which, crying bitterly, consumes itself in its own grief. Why do you abandon hope? Trust me and my wealth and the strength of my arm; I shall balance the scales of your fate. I promise you, you shall have your Layla. Even if she became a bird, escaping into the sky, even if she were a spark, deep inside the rock, I would still find her. I shall neither rest nor relax until I have married you to your moon-like love.'

When he heard these words, Majnun threw himself at his protector's feet. Soon, however, he became doubtful again and objected:

'Your words fill my soul with a delicious scent, but how do I know whether they are more than words, whether they are free from deception, whether you will act as you speak and whether you are even capable of acting? You ought to know that her mother, her parents, will never agree to give her in marriage to a man such as I, to a deranged one. "What?" they will say, "Are we to entrust this flower to the wind? Shall we allow a devil's child to play with a ray of the moon, hand over our daughter to a madman? Never!" Ah, you do not know these people yet as I do. Others have tried before to help me, but what was the use? Whatever they did, however hard they tried, my black fate did not become any whiter. Silver was offered in gleaming heaps, but it did not lighten the dark carpet of my days. So, you can see how hopeless my position is. To succeed would not be a human achievement, it would be a miracle. But I fear that you will soon have enough of this kind of hunting and turn back halfway, before you can trap your prey.

'Be it not so. And, if you really keep your promise,

may God reward you; but if you have only talked, showing me a *fata Morgana*, instead of an oasis, then, I implore you, rather tell me now and let me go on my way.'

This courageous speech strengthened Nawfal's friendly feelings towards the youth, who was of his own age, and he exclaimed:

'You doubt my word? All right, I shall make a pact with you. In the name of Allah the Almighty and his prophet Mohammed I swear that I shall fight for you and your cause like a wolf, no, like a lion, with my sword and all my resources.

'I solemnly vow that I shall enjoy neither food nor sleep until your heart's desire has been fulfilled... but you, in turn, must also promise me something—that you will show patience. Give up your frenzy, take your wild heart in hand, quieten it, tame it, if only for a few days.

'So let us seal our alliance; you damp down the fire in your heart, I in turn will open the iron gate to your treasure. Do you agree?'

Majnun consented. He smoothed the stormy sea of his soul and accepted his friend's helping hand. For the first time in many months, peace returned to his tortured mind, the marks inflicted by the branding iron of his madness began to heal. He trusted Nawfal like a child. And as peace came to his heart so a change came over his whole life. Without a word he abandoned the cave and accompanied his noble patron on horseback to his camp.

In the shade and protection of his powerful friend, as his confidant and guest, Majnun—by now no longer a 'majnun'—soon reverted to his old state as Qays, the beautiful and noble youth he had once been. He bathed and donned the fine garments and the turban which Nawfal had presented to him; he ate with pleasure, drank wine as a friend among friends and recited his qasidas and ghazals, not, as before, to the wind and the clouds, but to the hunters and warriors in their tents.

Fresh color flowed back into the yellow, wasted face, his bent figure became erect and he walked among his new companions, swaying like a tall reed in the wind. The flower, shorn of its leaves by the storm, was in bloom again. How greatly had he changed for the world, and the world for him. Since his return to the dwelling-places of men, nature had once more acquired a lovely face in the mirror of his eyes. The morning's gold-hemmed, festive attire delighted him as if he were seeing it for the first time, he joined in the midday laughter of the sun and had the colorful riddles of the roses explained to him. Yes, he had become a man among men again.

Nobody was happier about this change than Nawfal, who had brought it about. He was like a rain-carrying cloud, spreading its pearly showers over the summer-dry earth. Every day he brought new presents for his

recovering friend. Nothing was good or precious
enough. Majnun had to be at his side all the time and
Nawfal became so used to his company that he
refused to be parted even for an hour. The few days
which Nawfal had mentioned turned into as many
months. Their happiness lasted a long time—but now
thunderstorms were gathering on the horizon.

XVII

ONE day Majnun and Nawfal were sitting
together, gay and happy as usual. Who
would have thought that a bitter drop could fall into
the cup of their friendship? Suddenly a shadow
passed over Majnun's face, the smile on his lips died
and he recited these lines:

> *My sighs, my bitter tears leave you unmoved!*
> *My griefs and sorrows do not harass you.*
> *Not one, not half a promise did you keep*
> *Of many hundreds I received from you.*
> *You promised to fulfil my keen desire,*
> *Yet you forgot to grant my sweet reward!*
> *Instead of damping it, you stirred the fire,*
> *With empy words did you seduce my heart.*

Nawfal understood the meaning only too well. What
could he answer? The great warrior had no weapon
against this attack. He sat there, abashed, his lowered

eyes sad and melancholy. Majnun was more than ever overwhelmed by the desire for his beloved. It did not matter to him how hard it was: Nawfal had to fulfil what he had promised. In great bitterness Majnun continued:

'At the time when we made our covenant, your tongue was certainly very quick. Remember? Why then do you remain silent today? Why do you not offer a salve for my wounded heart? My patience is at an end, my reason rebels. Help me, lest I perish! Or must I seek assistance from better friends than you? What am I to think of you, a prince, who gives his word only to break it—and to me, friendless, weak, broken, dying of thirst for the water of life! Is it not one of the commandments, that one must offer water to the thirsty? Stand by your promise, or the madman whom you lured out of the desert will return to it. Unite me with Layla, or I shall throw my life away.'

XVIII

WHEN Nawfal heard his friend talking, his heart melted like wax in the flame. Without searching for words, where only deeds could count, he jumped up and went resolutely to work. Exchanging his robe for a suit of armor, he seized the sword instead of the cup and rallied a hundred horsemen, all skilled hunters and warriors, devoted to their chieftain and swift as birds of prey.

At the head of this army he set out, Majnun riding at his side, spoiling for the fray like a black lion. After a time they reached the pastures of Layla's tribe. When they could see the tents from afar, Nawfal ordered his men to dismount and pitch camp. Then he sent a herald to Layla's tribe with this message:

'I, Nawfal, have arrived with an army ready to fight you like an all-devouring fire. Hurry, therefore, and bring Layla to me; or the sword will have to decide between us. I am determined that Layla shall belong to the one man who is worthy of her, so that his longing may be stilled and his thirst quenched.'

After a while, the messenger returned with this reply:

'The way you have chosen will not lead you to your goal. Layla is no sweetmeat for people of your kind and to reach for the moon is not for everyone. The decision is not yours. Do you plan to steal the sun? Are you asking for the comets, you cursed demon? Draw your sword against us! You glassbottle, we shall know how to break you!'

Furious, Nawfal sent a second message:

'Ignorant fools, you do not seem to realize how keen is the edge of my sword! Once it has smitten you, you will never again worry about your racing dromedaries. Do you really think you can block the path of an ocean wave? Come, now! Do as you are told, or disaster will overtake you....'

But once more the herald returned with a rejection couched in abuse and derision. By now Nawfal was boiling with rage. He vented the red-hot fury of his heart in wild threats. He tore his sword out of its scabbard and led his men like a hungry lion towards the enemy camp. There also the men had prepared for battle. Bristling with arms they left the tents and soon the armies met in a terrible clash, like two mountains hurled at each other.

What noise, what uproar, what turmoil! The heavy breakers of battle rolled to and fro. While the cries of the warriors were rising to heaven, blood poured from their wounds into the thirsty sand. The swords became the cupbearers and filled the cups so overfull that the earth was drunk with purple-colored wine. Like lion's claws the spears tore breasts and limbs, the arrows drank the sap of life with wide open beaks like birds of prey; and proud heroes, heads severed from trunks, lay down for the sleep of eternity.

The thundering noise roaring over the battlefield deafened the dome of the sky and its stars. Steel and stone struck sparks, like the deadly lightning of fate. Like black wildcats, horseman set upon horseman—warriors crouching on their mounts as if riding white demons.

Majnun alone did not take part in this massacre. Was not death gathering the harvest for his sake? Yet he stood aside, his sword hidden in its sheath, though not from fear or cowardice. While each warrior thought of nothing but to kill the enemy and to defend himself, the poet was sharing the sufferings of both sides. Majnun was in deep torment. Every blow from friend or foe smote him. Unarmed, he threw himself into the middle of the fray, crying to God and to the fighting warriors for peace. Between the lines of battle he looked like a lonely pilgrim—but how could anyone take notice of him in such an hour? It was a miracle that he remained unharmed.

Did Majnun hope for Nawfal's victory? Indeed he should, but the longer the terrible fight lasted, the more confused became Majnun's heart. Had he not meant to die for Layla? Yet her own people, men of her tribe and blood, were now being killed for his sake! Killed by whom? By Nawfal and Nawfal's men, Majnun's friends!

Were they really his friends? Were they not rather his friends' enemies? Thus, while the battle of the horsemen raged outside, another struggle broke out inside the poet's soul, as bitter as the one in the field.

If shame had not paralysed his arm, Majnun would have drawn his sword against his own side. But he was conscious that this would be infamous. In his imagination he could hear the jeering laughter of the enemy, had he attacked from behind those whose only thought was to help him.

Still, if fate had permitted, he would have sent his arrows against those who fought Layla's tribe. His heart was with the men who defied his own champions. His lips prayed for help for his opponents. He longed to kiss the hand which had just flung one of Nawfal's riders out of the saddle.

In the end this impulse became so strong that he could hardly subdue it. Time and again he rejoiced when the enemy advanced, and became downcast and miserable when Nawfal's men gained an advantage.

Eventually one of Nawfal's horsemen noticed this. He turned to Majnun, shouting:

'What ails you, noble mind? Why do you enjoy this strife only from afar? Why do you even show favor to the enemy? Have you forgotten that we are risking our lives for you and for your sake?'

'If they were enemies,' Majnun replied, 'I could fight them. But as these enemies are my friends, what shall I do? This is no battlefield for me. The heart of my beloved beats for the enemy, and where her heart beats, there is my home. I want to die for my beloved, not kill other men. How then could I be on your side, when I have given up my self?'

Meanwhile Nawfal, sword in hand and constantly in the thick of battle, had striven hard for victory. Like the dare-devil he was, unflinching like a drunken elephant, he assailed time and again the walls of the enemy. Many of them he had struck down, but when the dark-blue tresses of the evening twilight began to throw their shadow over the day's burning forehead, the battle was still undecided. Soon night enveloped the fighting men. After the serpent of darkness had swallowed the last little glass pearl of light on the horizon, they separated, and soon none of them could see the others.

There were neither victors nor vanquished. But on both sides many brave men had fallen and the number of wounded was even greater than that of the dead. Nevertheless Nawfal had not given up hope of forcing the enemy to his knees on the following day. But when, in the first light of the new morning, he was about to lead his sadly diminished troop into battle, his scouts reported that during the night the enemy had been reinforced from other tribes.

If Nawfal was a hero, he was not a fool! After some reflection he decided on the only move still left to him. He sent a herald into the enemy camp with this message:

'Enough of the sword-play! Wounds have to be nursed; let us tread the way of peace. What I desired from you, and still desire, is the fairy-maid who could break the spell and free a bewitched youth from his delusion. In turn, I am prepared to pay you donkey-loads of treasure, and if you are ready to accept this proposal, your answer will sound much more harmonious than this my speech. But even if you refuse and your sugar is not for sale, we should nevertheless stop filling our lives with the sour taste of vinegar. Let the arms rest!'

The result was not unexpected. Nawfal's suggestion that Layla should be handed over against the payment of a huge sum was rejected with the same determination as on the day before. How could it have been otherwise? On the other hand there was no objection to a truce. No more blood was to be shed and Nawfal and his men returned home.

XIX

GONE were the beautiful days when Majnun, at Nawfal's side, had enjoyed life with his friends. The wound in the soul of our lover had opened again and he turned in bitterness against his friend.

He drew the sword of his tongue and spoke:

'Such then are your artful ways of uniting two lovers? Excellent indeed! Is that your wisdom's last resort, to raid with arms and men? Is that proof of your strength? Is that the key to your magic power? The masterpiece of your equestrian pride? Is that the way you throw the lasso? I certainly never wanted that. You have only succeeded in making enemies of my friends. The door through which I intended to enter, you have barred with a thousand locks. My good cause you have turned to bad; I herewith dissolve our friendship, my friend! Not the enemy—the friend has torn the thread; I am like the king in the game of chess, checkmated by his own knight; like the shepherd's dog, pierced by the arrow which his master aimed at the wolf.

'You may be great in your generosity, yet how small you are when it comes to fulfilling your promises.'

Nawfal found it hard to stand up to such words. He had to cover himself with his shield and at the same time try to cure his wounded opponent. 'You must understand,' he replied, 'the enemy was superior in numbers and in arms. That is why I was unable to win Layla—as yet. I made peace and retreated. But that was a trick forced on me by necessity. Be sure that I shall return! I am now assembling an army from all the tribes around us and you can be certain that I shall not rest until I have sunk my steel into this stone, until I have pulled this stubborn donkey from the roof down to the ground!'

And Nawfal meant what he said. He sent messengers to all the tribes from Medina to Baghdad. He opened wide his treasure chests; and after he had assembled an army that surged from horizon to horizon like an ocean of iron, he went once more to war in order to conquer Layla for his friend.

XX

ONE day, with kettledrums beating, the steel wave of Nawfals' army appeared in front of the tents of Layla's tribe. Man close to man, spear next to spear, line after line—the whole plain was full of them, as far as the eye could see. The horses' hoofbeats shook the earth, and the roar of the approaching host would have caused the heart of a dead man to tremble.

Nevertheless the brave defenders did not lose heart. They were still not willing to give way to force, determined not to hand over Layla to the madman and his helpers. They preferred to die rather than live under such a shameful yoke.

So battle was renewed. This time the clash between horses, men and arms was even more terrifying than before. So wedged and locked in battle became friend and foe that none could dodge the other, nor did thrust or stroke ever miss its victim.

Blood poured in streams from wounds and weapons as if it had to wash each grain of sand in the desert, and it looked as if red flowers were suddenly springing up from the arid soil.

At last the killing became too much. Even the most warlike hearts began to tire of inflicting pain, and the swords hesitated before they struck, as if ashamed of mowing down more and more heads.

Nawfal, the great warrior, fought again in the front line. Spitting fire and destruction like a dragon, he cut a man's life-thread with every breath, and step by step, smashed the rock-like enemy to pieces. What his club hit was certain to be crushed—even if it had been the mighty Elburz mountain; and whoever ventured within range of his sword had the book of his fate closed for all time.

Even before night could cover this bloodthirsty drama, the day had granted the flame of victory to Nawfal's men. The enemy retreated. Layla's tribe was defeated, many were killed, many wounded or near dead from exhaustion.

As a sign of submission and mourning, the elders sprinkled earth on their heads and started, as soon as the weapons fell silent, on the bitter path to the victor's tent. In front of Nawfal's threshold, they kissed the earth and lamented:

'You, Lord and Master, are the victor. We, your enemies, have been defeated—dead or alive. Now let justice prevail. Do not refuse peace to a few survivors! Allow us resurrection after our fall and remember that one day we shall all be faced with another resurrection. Put your sword back into its sheath; you no longer need it against the defenceless men who are lying here at your feet asking forgiveness. Let spears and arrows rest! Look, we have thrown away our shields and entrust our fate to your hands.'

Hearing the elders speak thus, Nawfal was moved by their grief. He too was ready to bury the past and granted the truce they requested without, however, forgetting to demand his price. 'Bring me the bride and that at once,' he ordered, 'then I shall be satisfied and leave you alone, you and your tribe.'

No sooner had he given this order, than a single man stepped out of the crowd of defeated tribesmen. It was Layla's father, bent low by sorrow. In great humility he · knelt before the victorious Nawfal, buried his forehead in the dust and filled the big tent with lamentation.

'Great Prince among the Arabs,' he began, 'look at me, an old man, broken-hearted, beaten down by disaster, and prostrate before you. The Arabs are heaping blame and infamy upon me, as if I were a homeless stranger, and when I think of the streams of blood which have been shed for my sake, I wish I could become a drop of quicksilver and escape from such disgrace....It is now your task to pronounce judgment. If you leave me my daughter, you can be certain of my gratitude. If you are determined to kill her—do! Cut her to pieces, burn her, drown her; I shall not rebel against your decision.

'One answer alone I will not accept; never shall I give

Layla to this demon, this Majnun, a madman who should be tied with iron bands, not with nuptial bonds. Who, after all, is he? A fool, a common muddle-head, a vagrant and homeless tramp, who roams mountains and steppes. And what has he ever achieved? Shall I sit down with a vile versifier who has sullied my good name—and his own? There is not one corner in the whole of Arabia where my daughter's name is not bandied about on everyone's lips—and I should give her to him who is the cause of all this? My name would be infamous forever. Do not demand the impossible! Woe to us if you insist! I swear to God that I would rather cut off her head with my own hands and feed this moon-like bride to the dogs—to save my honor and to live in peace....Better that the dogs should devour her than this demon in human shape. Better they than he!'

For a moment this daring speech and its terrible threat silenced Nawfal. But in his heart he forgave the old man and answered without rancor:

'Stand up! Even though I am the victor, I want you to give me your daughter only if you are willing. A woman taken by violence is like a slice of dry bread and a salty sweet.'

Thus he responded to Layla's father and it soon became clear that his confidants, who were present, agreed with him. It was Majnun's own doing. Had he not, during the first battle, taken the side of the enemy and in his heart become a traitor to his friends?

The horseman who had observed and then spoken to Majnun, now turned to Nawfal and said:

'The old man is right. This fool is full of impure lust. Rebellion dominates his mind and he is in no way fit to marry. He is unstable and completely unreliable. Didn't we fight to the death for his sake? Yet he hoped that the enemy would win. Haven't we, on his behalf, offered our bodies as a target for their arrows? Meanwhile he blessed these arrows behind our backs! Is that the way for a man in his senses to behave? He cries and laughs without rhyme or reason. Even if he should win his beloved, fate would not favor their union....He is full of faults, and you, Nawfal, will come to feel ashamed that you once helped him. Better to be content with the shame and honor we have already won and wash our hands of this affair.'

This turned the scale. What was Nawfal to do? Although defeated, Layla's father remained inexorable. And Nawfal's own men supported him! Nawfal could not even blame them. Did not doubts prey upon his own mind? Was there not truth in what Layla's father and Nawfal's men said?

Nawfal decided to forgo the price of victory and gave order to break camp.

XXI

THEY had not gone far before Majnun turned his horse towards Nawfal. His eyes streaming with tears, he boiled over with rage like a volcano.

'Faithless friend,' he shouted, 'you let my hopes ripen into a radiant dusk and now you push me into the daylight of despair. Why, tell me, did your hand drop its prey? What has happened to this arm once ready to help me? When I was thirsty you led me to the banks of the Euphrates, but before I could drink you dragged me back into my desert hell. You brought sugar out of your box to make sherbet, but you did not offer it to me. You placed me in front of a table laden with sweetmeats, and then you chased me away like a fly!

'As you never intended to let me have my treasure, it would have been better not to show it to me....' Majnun turned his horse without waiting for an answer and galloped into the pathless wilderness, away from Nawfal and his friends. He disappeared from their sight like a cloud which consumes itself, like the rain of tears which fell from his eyes, leaving no trace in the sand.

When Nawfal had returned to his hunting grounds and there was still no sign of Majnun, he went with a few men to look for him. He was devoted to his friend and anxious to comfort him, but in spite of long and strenuous efforts, they could find no trace of Majnun. It was as if his name had been erased from the book of life, and Nawfal began to fear that he had lost his friend for ever.

XXII

AFTER he had left Nawfal, Majnun sped away on his horse like a bird without a nest—far into the desert, only the wind as his companion. Singing to himself about Nawfal's unfaithfulness, he told his unhappy fate to the half-effaced traces of abandoned resting-places and campfires.

Suddenly he discovered some dots moving in the distance. When he came nearer he found a strange group confronting him. Two gazelles had been caught in snares and a hunter was just about to kill the poor creatures with his dagger.

'Let these animals go free!' shouted Majnun, 'I am your guest and you can't refuse my request. Remove the nooses from their feet! Is there not room enough in this world for all creatures? What have these two done that you are bent on killing them? Or are you a wolf, not a human being, that you want to take the burden of such a sin upon yourself? Look how beautiful they are! Are their eyes not like those of the beloved? Does their sight not remind you of the spring? Let them go free, leave them in peace! These necks are too good for your steel, these breasts and thighs are not meant to be devoured, these backs, which have never carried any burden, are not destined for your fire!'

Never before had the hunter heard anything like this. His mouth opened in astonishment, then he began to chew one of his fingers. Finally, when he had regained his composure, he replied:

'I have heard what you said. But look, I am poor, otherwise I would gladly obey you. This is the first catch I have made for two months. I have a wife and children: do you expect me to spare the animals and let my family starve?'

Without a word Majnun jumped out of the saddle and handed the reins of his horse to the hunter who, well content with the exchange, mounted and rode away, leaving Majnun alone with the two gazelles. Gently kissing their eyes Majnun sang:

> *Dark as the night, like hers, your eyes!*
> *What I have lost you can't return.*
> *They waken memories that burn,*
> *Sad happiness and joyful sighs.*

Blessing the animals, he freed them from their fetters and watched them disappear towards the horizon. Then he continued on his way, only much slower, bent under the weight of his grief and his few possessions. The sand scorched his feet and the sun blazed down on his head. His brain seemed to boil, thorns tore his garments; but he did not seem to notice and pursued his way until night covered day with a blue-black shroud, and the moon rose, borrowing its lustre from the sun.

Only then did the lonely wanderer halt. He crept into a cave groaning like a lizard which has been bitten by a serpent, and scattered the pearls of his tears into the tresses of darkness. Sighing he crouched under the rock and read page after page from the book of his life, whose leaves were as black as the hours of the night which dwindled away without allowing him any sleep.

XXIII

WHEN the morning, lighting up the world, unfolded its banner and the sun, rising in China, ascended in the sky, the nocturnal ghosts released Majnun's mind. Like smoke rising from the fire he emerged from his hiding place and continued on his way, composing poems and singing them aloud to himself.

Towards evening he came upon another hunter who had caught a stag in his snares and was about to kill it. Majnun ran quickly towards him and shouted, his voice as sharp as the spike of a bloodletter:

'You hyena of a tyrant! Torturer of the weak and the defenseless! Release this poor creature at once so that it may still enjoy its life for a short while. How will the hind feel tonight without her companion? What would she say if she could talk with a human tongue! She would exclaim: "May he who has done this to us, suffer as we do; may he never see another happy day! ..." Would you like that? Do you not fear the distress of those who suffer? Imagine yourself as the stag—the stag as the hunter and you as his victim!'

'It is not important to kill the stag,' replied the trapper, 'what matters to me is to sustain my own life. I have caught the animal, but if you wish, I am willing to sell it to you.'

Majnun had no treasure, but he was still carrying a few things which Nawfal had given him. He laid them at the feet of the hunter who was well satisfied with the bargain. Loading them on to his shoulders he said farewell and left the stag with Majnun.

When he had gone, Majnun approached the animal as gently as a father his child. Stroking and caressing it, he said:

'Like myself, are you not also separated from your beloved? Quick-footed runner of the steppes, dweller of the mountains, how vividly you remind me of her! Go, hurry, search for her, your mate. Rest in her shadow—there is your place. And if in your wanderings you should pass Layla's tent, perhaps even encounter her, give her this message from me:

> *I am yours, however distant you may be!*
> *Your sorrow, when you grieve, brings grief to me.*
> *There blows no wind but wafts your scent to me,*
> *There sings no bird but calls your name to me.*
> *Each memory that has left its trace with me*
> *Lingers for ever, as if part of me.*

'Tell her that, my friend!'

With these words Majnun removed the noose from the legs of the stag and set it free while, high above, the caravan of the night went on its way and in the eastern sky the moon emerged from the darkness. Foaming like the waters of the Nile, the Milky Way seemed to flow across this celestial Egypt—while Majnun, left alone, looked up to the sky like a bird with clipped wings, erect like a candle which stands upright as it burns away.

XXIV

THE dawn of a new day spread its radiant yellow light between the spokes of heaven's night-blue wheel, while the awakening sun painted fresh red roses on the horizon. But Majnun was like a flower in autumn. Beaten down by grief and exhaustion his head drooped and when, towards noon, the sun shot its arrows at him, he was happy to find a small oasis where, under some palm trees, a spring was bubbling and a pool invited the wanderer to rest. Water and greenery and shade! This place, thought Majnun, is like a corner of Paradise which has fallen down to earth; like an image of the fields around the celestial lake Kowthar.

Having drunk his fill, he lay down on the brocade carpet of soft grass in the shade of the palm trees to rest awhile.

Soon the tired man was wrapped in peaceful slumber. Time passed unnoticed. When he woke, the sun was already low in the west. He had the feeling that someone had been staring at him. But who? No living soul was visible, far or near.

By chance, his eye fell on the crown of the date-palm in whose shade and protection he had rested. There, in the green trelliswork of the fan-shaped branches, he saw a black shadow: a big raven squatted motionless, staring at Majnun, eyes glowing like lamps.

Dressed in mourning, he is a wanderer like myself, thought Majnun, and in our hearts we probably feel the same. Aloud he said to the bird:

'Blackfrock, for whom are you mourning? Why this sombre color of the night in the light of day? Are you burning in the fire of my grief, or have I disguised my soul with your blackness?'

When the raven heard the voice, he hopped on to another branch without taking his eyes off Majnun who continued:

'If you, like myself, belong to those whose hearts have been burned, why do you shun me? Or are you a Khatib, who on Fridays preaches from the pulpit of a mosque? Is that why you are wearing this sombre garb? Or are you a negro watchman? If so, whom do you fear? Perhaps I am a shah and you are my princely protector? Heed not! If, in your flight, you happen to see my beloved, tell her this from me:

> *Help me, oh help me in my loneliness!*
> *Lonely my lightfades in the wilderness.*
> *'Be not afraid, for I am yours,' you said,*
> *Do not delay—lest you should find me dead.*
> *Caught by the wolf, the lamb hears all too late*
> *The shepherd's flute lament its cruel fate.*
> *Dying from thirst, I search the sky in vain—*
> *Too late the cloud that brings the saving rain.*

As Majnun recited these lines, the raven fluttered farther and farther away until he finally took wing from the crown of the palm tree, vanishing into the fading light, which seemed to swallow him up.

It was no longer day, but not yet night: the hour of the bats' awakening. The darkness grew until it was as black as a raven's plumage. What a giant raven this night was. When its wings were spread they reached right across the sky and yellow ravens' eyes stared down on Majnun as before, only now there were thousands of them, great and small, a countless multitude.

To hide from their gaze, Majnun covered his face with his hands, and wept bitterly.

XXV

WHEN the light of the morning pushed its head through the curtain of the night, the old world came to life afresh in every creature's eyes—like a new garden.

Majnun could no longer endure to be so far from his beloved. He hurried along as if he had grown raven's wings overnight, or like a butterfly rushing through the darkness towards the flame which it seeks to encircle.

The closer he came to his goal, the more his heart became drunk with Layla's scent, the louder his ears perceived the sound of her voice, the clearer his eyes recognized her face in mountains and valleys.

All strength seemed to have gone from his limbs and he had to take rest; he was like a man who has dwelt for a long time among the dead and now with every breath, with every sigh, feels the stream of life slowly returning.

While he sat there, two strange figures approached. A woman dragged a man behind her—his hair and beard dishevelled, his limbs weighed down by iron chains so heavy that he could hardly walk; he looked and behaved as if out of his senses, and the woman tugged constantly on the rope hurrying him along like an ox or a donkey.

Majnun, deeply shocked, felt pity for the poor man. He implored the woman not to use her prisoner so roughly and asked: 'Who is this man? What has he done that you drag him around chained like that?'

'Do you want to hear the truth?' said the woman. 'All right then. He is neither crazy nor a criminal. I am a widow and he is a dervish, both of us have suffered great hardship. We are both ready to do anything if only we can fill purse and belly. That is why I decided to parade him in chains, hoping that people would think him mad and give us food and alms out of charity. What we receive, we divide fairly between us.'

When Majnun heard these words, he went down on his knees and beseeched her:

'Relieve this man of his chains and put them on me. I am one of those unhappy men with a disturbed mind. I should be tied up—not he. Take me with you as long and wherever you wish and everything that is given to us shall be yours.

The old woman did not wait to be told twice. Quickly

she freed the dervish from his chains, tying up Majnun in his stead. He was as pleased as if she had caressed him and she walked on happily, leading her new victim by the rope.

Whenever the woman and her prisoner came to a tent, they stopped: Majnun recited his love poems, cried out 'Layla ... Layla ...,' banged head and body against the stones, and, in spite of his chains, danced around like a drunken madman, while the woman punished him.

One day they came to an oasis where a few tents had been erected. Looking at them more closely, Majnun suddenly recognized Layla's tent among them. Tears began to stream from his eyes like floods of rainwater pouring from the clouds in spring. He collapsed, hit his head against the ground and called out:

'You have left me to myself, sharing with me nothing but your grief. Look, I am doing penance because I made you and your people suffer under the hands of Nawfal. As a punishment I have given up my freedom. Shackled I stand before you, a rope around my neck, waiting to be chastised. I know I have sinned, and my sin is so great that it can never be forgiven.

'I am your prisoner; you be my judge. Condemn me! Punish me as severely as you like....It is my fault that your people have suffered. In expiation I am beating my body with my own hands. Yesterday I committed my crime, today I have returned in chains to suffer torture from you. Kill me, but do not reject me in my misery. How can I plead innocence in front of you? You are loyal, even when you have abandoned loyalty; I am guilty, even when I am innocent.

'In life, your greetings did not reach me, and your hands did not stroke my hair. But now there is hope. Maybe you will look at me while you kill me with your arrow, and then put your hand on my head? Maybe you will draw your sword, allowing me to rest my head on your threshold like an animal to be sacrificed? I will be as trusting as Ismael before Abraham! Why should I be afraid, if it is you who cuts off my head? My heart burns like a candle—if you cut the wick, it burns even brighter! As long as I am alive there is no way that could lead me to you; save yourself, therefore, save me from myself, and let me rest at your feet in eternal peace.'

Majnun could say no more. With a loud cry he flew from the ground like an arrow, his face insanely contorted. Raving as if possessed by a demon, he seized his chains in both hands, and, in a superhuman effort, tore them apart; striking himself in the face, he raced away from the old woman, from Layla's tent, from all human beings—towards the mountainous wastes of Najd.

His parents, his relatives and friends, were told. They had already heard what had happened to him during the last weeks and months. Some searched for him, but when they found him in one of his hiding places in the mountains, they realized that the past, apart from Layla's name and memory, had been extinguished from his mind. As soon as they tried to talk of anything else, he fell silent, or escaped, withdrawing into himself, as if drunk with sleep. These attempts only excited him, but led nowhere, and so, in the end, even his father and mother had to abandon hope that he would ever recover and return to them.

XXVI

WHAT, in the meantime, had happened to Layla? Hear what the deep-sea diver sounding the ocean of the soul has to tell you!

Layla soon learned of Nawfal's victory—and it was her father who told her. He came rushing into the tent, covered in dust and blood, battered and exhausted, his turban awry.

Yet, he did not look like a man in need of comfort after shameful defeat. He was tired, but his eyes shone with satisfaction and his voice sounded triumphant. 'What a master-stroke,' he said proudly. 'I have managed to tame this man Nawfal with my tongue, after his sword had beaten us! I have escaped disaster by the breadth of a hair! This maniac, this Majnun, almost forced his way in— and then what would have happened? Now Nawfal, who fought in God's name and won—may heaven reward him—has withdrawn. We are saved.'

Layla had to listen, although her heart was almost breaking with grief; but while her father and other people were present, she dared not show it.

Secretly she wept and suffered and, when the night hid her from prying eyes, she allowed her tears to fall freely until her sleepless eyes were red-rimmed like those of the narcissus.

Her parents' home had become her prison. Guarding the secret of her love, which must not be revealed, she lived like a serpent, unable to find a way out of a tightly fastened bag. She waited, listening to the wind, as it lovingly caressed the tent, hoping it might bring a message from her beloved.

Meanwhile, Majnun's poems extolling Layla's beauty and recounting the story of their love had spread among the tribes, and noble suitors came from far and near to try their luck. One offered land, another sheep, yet another gold; full of desire, they used every trick and art of persuasion to reach their goal.

But, whatever treasures they had to offer, no matter how strongly they insisted, flattered and implored, Layla's father remained unmoved. With great care, he protected the glass so that no stone should break it, and barred the door which led to the girl with the silvery limbs.

When he was present, Layla drank the wine of gaiety—when he turned his back, she ate the bread of grief. She was a candle which smiles through tears, a rose which hides her thorns, a lame girl supported by the arms of her parents, who thought she was walking unaided.

Ibn Salam had, of course, also heard about the hordes of suitors perilously encircling his promised jewel. His impatience and desire became inflamed by fear until he could stand it no longer. He equipped a caravan worthy of a king. With donkey-loads of amber, musk, jewels and sweetmeats of all kinds, he started off, hoping to conquer the treasure with treasures. He scattered gold coins among the people like so many grains of sand, and his camels, buried under the load of silken garments, looked like walking hills of brocade.

When he arrived, Ibn Salam allowed himself and his men two days of rest, then he sent his mediator to Layla's family. This man was a master of his art. He could weave a magic spell with words, and make a stone melt with shame. So great was his eloquence that, like the Messiah, he could have breathed life into a corpse.

Layla's father could not resist such determined assault; and even less, when the orator with infectious enthusiasm displayed before delighted eyes treasures from the towns of Araby, from China and Byzantium as presents, using the key of his sweet tongue to open the lock which was already giving way.

'Consider,' he said to Layla's father, 'what kind of a man is this Ibn Salam, a knight like a lion, backbone of any army, pride of the Arabs! Not only his sword, but untold numbers of men obey him; wherever he goes, his name races ahead of him, and his honor is without a flaw. If it must be, he will shed blood like water and gold like sand. Who would not accept such a mighty warrior as his son-in-law? If you are in need of reliable men—he will find them. If you are in need of protection—he will grant it.'

Like rain in springtime, which never seems to stop, the words poured over Layla's father, who had hardly a chance to open his mouth. What could he do, what could he say? Had he not already promised his daughter to Ibn Salam? True, he would have preferred to wait even longer; events still went too fast for him. Yet, however much he turned and twisted, searching for excuses—as a man, surprised by the enemy, searches for his arms—his skilled opponent drove him into a corner with the sword of his tongue, until, in the end, he had to surrender, handing over his moon into the jaws of the dragon.

The day of the marriage was fixed. When it dawned, and the sun covered the shoulders of the night with her prayer-mat, woven from early light—just as one bedecks the shoulders of a bridegroom—Layla's father went to work. Ibn Salam, his entourage and the other guests were led into the festival tent, where everything had been sumptuously prepared for their reception. As is the Arabian custom, the guests were sitting together, admiring the bride's presents, throwing a tufan of silver coins into the air, enjoying choice delicacies and weaving new ties between the families on either side, talking and joking, in laughter and gaiety.

And Layla? The women, while adorning the rooms, burning scented aloe wood and sprinkling it with sugar, never noticed the bride's tears, bitter as rosewater and hot as fire. Among all these gay people, Layla alone was sad. Never had she been so lonely, so desperate. Was not everything now lost? How close she and Majnun had been to their goal! But the goblet had cracked just as their lips touched its rim.

Nobody here had an inkling of what was happening in Layla's heart. Who notices the thorn which makes you limp when you try to run? A lame foot does not obey orders. Those who rebel against their own tribe, lose the tribe. A finger bitten by a snake must be cut off. Life is built on the harmony of all its elements; when this harmony is disturbed, death moves into the breach. And however much people enjoyed her beauty, Layla carried death in her soul.

XXVII

NEXT morning, when, with all resplendent stars aboard, the vessel of the night had speeded down the Tigris river of the sky and the sun once more pitched her shining tent on the blue meadow, Ibn Salam, too, gave his caravan the signal to start. How happy he was. He had left his treasures behind, and his beasts of burden were returning without their loads, but what did all the treasures of Arabia mean to him beside the jewel which he had won?

He had a litter prepared for Layla—richer outside, or softer within, none could be imagined. Carried by camels, honored and served like a princess, she made the journey from the tents of her tribe to those in the realm of her husband.

When they arrived Ibn Salam said to her: 'Everything you can see is yours. My possessions are yours, my Kingdom is yours.'

But how did Layla reward him for his kindness? Well, the days passed and the shadow which had begun to cloud the happiness in his heart increased and darkened. Who would feel differently if the woman of his passionate desire refused to share his bed when, after long pursuit, he had finally won her and brought her home as his wife? Ibn Salam was left with nothing but hope and patience. Waiting from night to night, he tried, during the day, to read every wish in the eyes of his beloved, yet, when darkness fell, he was left once more sleepless and alone.

Why? he thought; is she not my wife? Why should I not take what is mine? Long enough have I tried to melt this wax with kindness—perhaps force will achieve what is refused to gentleness? Perhaps that is what she expects.

Action followed thought. Ibn Salam stretched out his hands towards the garden, determined to pluck from the palm tree the date which was not granted willingly.

But alas! Instead of the fruit he felt the thorn, instead of sweetness he tasted bitter gall. Before he even knew whet was happening to him, the gardener hit him so hard that he went nearly deaf and blind.

'If you try once more,' said Layla, 'you will regret it for your sake and for mine. I have sworn an oath to my creator that I will not give in to you. You can shed my blood with your sword, but you cannot take me by force.'

Ibn Salam was deeply in love with Layla—therefore he gave in to her wish. He said to himself: 'Even if she does not love me, I would rather be allowed to look at her than not to possess her at all. As it is, I can at least glance at her from time to time, otherwise I would lose her for good.'

He went even further and, like a poor sinner, humbled himself, asking forgiveness for having tried to use force.

'My heart is content, even if I am only allowed to look at you. I would be a common thief if I asked for more.'

So it was, and so it remained.

While Ibn Salam's eyes searched for Layla, hers looked only for Majnun, or for a sign from him. Might not a breath of wind bring a speck of dust from his mountain cave? As if drunk, Layla would sometimes take two or three steps, stumbling to the entrance of the tent. There her soul, sadder than a thousand love-songs, would escape for a while, so that she could forget herself. She lived only in thoughts of Majnun, hoping for a message from him.

XXVIII

MEANWHILE, Majnun was like a man who leaves the ruins of his home and village and, never settling down, wanders from place to place, alone but for the echo of his grief.

A year had passed since Layla's marriage to Ibn Salam, and still Majnun had not even heard of it. He was a wanderer who did not see where he was going, drunk with the wafting scent of love; the scent of a whole springtime is as nothing compared with it. Melancholia had colored his body amber yellow and against such illness there grows on earth no healing herb.

One evening, Majnun was again lying exhausted in the desert under a blossoming thorn-bush. Thorns and blossoms were only a blur before his burning eyes. He neither saw nor heard the rider who, traveling through the dusk of the steppe on his tired camel, came nearer and nearer, like a poisonous snake, stealthily stalking its victim.

The rider, whose skin was black as a negro's, had espied the man lying under the thorn-bush, and realized who he was. A few steps away he halted his mount and scathing words penetrated Majnun's unhappy ears, like the voice of a demon.

'Oho, you there, who does not know what is going on in the world, you idolater! Truly it would be better for you to turn your back on your beloved. Do you still expect her to be faithful to you? You fool! Do you still hope for light, where there is darkness? What, from afar, seems to you a shining beacon, is a delusion. You are acting stupidly. A mistress like yours is worse than none!'

Then the stranger shouted even more harshly:

'She deceives you, don't you understand? The

woman to whom you have entrusted your heart, has handed it over to the enemy. Your seed has been scattered to the wind, and Layla has forgotten you. She has been given in marriage to another man, and, believe me, she did not refuse him. Oh no! Every night she sleeps in his arms: she thinks only of kissing and making love and swoons in sensual pleasure while you torture and exhaust yourself. Is that right? Look at the abyss which separates you! Do as she does. Think of her no longer, just as she no longer thinks of you!'

And ever deeper the black devil buried his poison fang in Majnun's soul:

'Did you believe her to be the one and only among thousands, different from all others? Ha! That is what women are like, fickle and faithless from beginning to end. One like all, and all like one. For a while she looks upon you as a hero, and then, all at once, you are nobody. True, they are full of passion, even more than we, but they pursue only their own selfish interests. Women are cheats! There is deceit and hypocrisy in everything they do. Never trust a woman! She will repay you with torture. And rightly so! A man who believes in women's fidelity, is even more stupid than she who makes him suffer. What, after all, is a woman? A dustbin of falsity and viciousness; peace, when you look at her from outside, and turmoil within. As your enemy she stirs up trouble with the whole world, as your friend she corrupts your soul. If you tell her: 'Do this!'—it is certain that she will not. If you say, 'Don't do it!'—she will risk her life to do it. Happy when you suffer, she is eaten by grief when you rejoice. That is woman's way, that and even worse. Remember!'

So the black-faced one spoke, and there arose a moan of despair from the bottom of Majun's heart. Like a bird dropping out of the sky fatally wounded, Majnun's head dropped, striking the stones so hard that his spurting blood colored the earth red. His body, in tattered rags, twisted and writhed. Then his soul spread its nightwings and fled; mercifully a faint veiled his limbs.

The rider watched. Whether man or demon—he was seized by pity. Ashamed and no longer proud of the magic power of his words, he jumped from the saddle and waited near the thorn-bush until the lover's soul returned to his wretched body. Then he broke into a thousand pleas for forgiveness.

'Listen to me,' he clamored, 'listen; what I just told you was a lie, a wicked lie. A bad joke it was, nothing more. I have turned the truth inside out. Layla has not deceived nor betrayed you, nor has she forgotten you. Broken-hearted, her face veiled, she suffers behind the curtain of her tent—longing for you. Her husband? Is he really her husband, he with whom she has never yet shared her bed? Although married to him, she has remained faithful to you, Majnun. She has no one else in this world, and not a moment passes when she does not think of you a hundred times. More than a year has gone by since her marriage and still Layla, chaste as ever, lives only in her love for you....What is a year, after all? If a hundred, even a thousand, years separated you—it is inconceivable that Layla would ever forget Majnun.

Majnun listened to these words. Were they true? Certainly they soothed the agony of his heart. At last he could weep, and the tears streaming down his worn face into the dust made him look like a bird with broken wings. He had nowhere on earth to rest his head; even the verses which came from his lips were lost, like his tears, because she, for whom they were meant, was far away.

XXIX

MAJNUN was shaken to the depths of his being. Before his eyes he saw the dream face of his beloved; the flame of his longing tempted him to join her. He stumbled on his way like a bird dragging its wings in the dust. His grief had made him as light as a hair, and it was hard to believe that there was a breath of life left in his body. Desperately longing to speak to Layla, but unable to reach her, he engaged the wind as his messenger, and many were the verses he sent to her.

The wind obligingly carried his lines away, but

response there was none. Bitter is the wine of lonely
love, yet, if sometimes in his grief Majnun doubted
Layla, his own passion did not abate. So he went on
singing:

> *You torture me to death, yet while I live*
> *Your beauty makes me love you and forgive,*
> *I am the lamp, you are the sun—your might*
> *Conquers triumphantly my waning light.*
> *Your radiant eyes the fire envies you,*
> *Tulips and roses fade when meeting you.*
> *Be parted? Never! Kneeling I confess*
> *Love and devotion, faithful unto death.*
> *Tormented I endure, resigned, your blows:*
> *Yours, if I die, will be the blood that flows.*

XXX

IT is a long time since we have spoken of
Majnun's father, the old Sayyid. Had he not done
everything that a father could do for his son? In his
grief he was like Jacob after Joseph had been taken
from him; but Jacob had other sons; not so the
Sayyid.

Age and sorrow had bent his back. He could clearly
see his fate, as black as a negro, who never becomes
a white tartar though he be washed ever so often. For
days and nights he sat in a corner of his tent, waiting
for the sign of departure to his last resting place. He

knew only too well that it could not be long delayed and that the signposts erected for him were 'Old Age,' 'Weakness' and 'Sorrow'. There was only one tie still binding him to this earth. He was not afraid of death, but he did not want to leave without setting eyes on his child for the last time. Earthly possessions meant little to him, but to leave them to a stranger instead of his son pained him. He was determined to seek out Majnun, to talk to him once more, and perhaps—who knows?—rescue his soul from its obsession, to tear his heart from the desert.

This hope gave the old man greater strength than one would have thought possible. Again he set out for Majnun's sake, his tired body supported by a staff, accompanied by two youths from his tribe, and confident that the Almighty would come to his aid.

He traversed vast plains, scorched by the heat of the sun, he crossed lonely mountain passes beneath towering peaks; his feet sank into oceans of sand, he rested in the green island shade of many an oasis and hopefully asked every passing stranger for news of his lost son. For a long time his search was fruitless. At last, when his feet would carry him no longer, a Bedouin said to him:

'Majnun? I know where he is! A terrible spot, a place of anguish, a cave in the desert like a tomb, right in the flames of Hell.... Don't go there!'

But the old man insisted and, after a last day's

journey, reached his goal. His goal? One would not wish anybody to find himself in a place so deserted, so bleak and harrowing that it made the heart quail—there he found his son.

Was this really his son? This creature hardly resembling a human being, a living skeleton, almost beyond this world, secluded like a hermit, immersed in idolatry, separated by only a hair's breadth from the land of death, with the flail already swinging over his head. He moved on all fours over the ground like an animal; or was he perhaps already one of those ghosts from the lower regions who appear and vanish in many strange shapes? Then again he writhed like a serpent, bare-headed, naked, except for a scrap of leather round his loins.

His perturbed spirit had left the ruin of his body, and dwelt so far away that he did not even recognize the visitor. When the old Sayyid set eyes on his son, he fell on his knees, overwhelmed by love and sorrow. He laid his hand on the unhappy boy's head; tenderly he caressed his hair and his forehead, while tears, like rain, streamed down his cheeks. Then only did Majnun lift his eyes. He looked at his father—yet did not see him. Who was this? Someone weeping! Weeping—for whom? Majnun stared into his father's face without recognizing him. He had forgotten himself. How then could he remember anyone else? He turned his head and murmured:

'Who are you? What do you want with me? Where do

you come from?'

The old man replied: 'I have been looking for you all
the time.'

When Majnun heard this voice, he suddenly
recognized his father. Putting his head on the old
man's knee, he sobbed uncontrollably, then they fell
into each other's arms, weeping and kissing, again
and again; for a long time they stayed holding each
other in close embrace.

When the storm had abated, the father became even
more distressed about the appearance of his son. Did
he not look like one of the dead, resurrected in
nakedness from the grave on the day of the Last
Judgment? Something must be done! Quickly the
Sayyid took from his travelling bag a cloak of the
finest linen, also shoes and a turban. What did
Majnun care about these things? He put them on in
obedience to his father.

'Soul of your father,' said the old man. 'What place is
this where to rest your head? Is this where you are
hiding? Do you want to wait here for the arrow of a
cruel fate, to be devoured by wild beasts when you
have died? I implore you, escape while there is time!
Truly, with us a stray dog has a better life than you.
Have you run so far in order to find this place?
Believe me, you can run all your life without arriving
anywhere. You will only get more tired, more weary.
What use is all this agony? Whom does it help? Do

you want to be the bed of a stream whose banks are burst by the floods? A mountain, split by an earth tremor? You must overcome your grief, otherwise it will devour you even if you be of iron. You have been a rebel all this time.

'Enough! Learn to accept this world as it is. Stop living in the wilderness like a beast among beasts; do not hide in mountain caves, a versifying demon, a leech sucking its own blood! Try to be patient, think of something else, even of trifling pleasures. Tempt yourself, be gay and happy, joke and dally; anything—be it as fleeting as a breath of wind. Why not? That is life; whether its promises are true or false, enjoy what the moment brings. What is of lasting value in this world? Enjoy what you have—today; and eat what you have harvested —now! Never trust tomorrow. Your day is today. How do we know? Tomorrow death may hold the reins. What use then to regret? Nothing counts but what you have achieved. A woman wears only what she has woven; a man reaps only what he has sown. If you hope one day to win renown, begin today. Behave as if your life were in the hands of Death even now—then, when he comes, you will not have to worry. Only those who die their own death can hope to escape his claws.'

Hopefully the old man continued:

'Does not all sorrow come to an end? Does not even a dog have a home? You are human, therefore live

like a man! Or are you a ghoul, a demon of the desert
in human shape? Even then, you should live like a
man or return to the underworld. Oh my son! Be my
companion for the few days which still remain: for
me, night is falling. If today you turn away, tomorrow
you will look for me in vain. I have to go and you
must take over my task. Soon my sufferings will be
ended, but you should be happy! Look, my sun is
sinking, darkened by the haze of a long day. Dusk is
waiting for me, my son—my soul is taking wing.
Come then, come! Do not delay. Take my place,
which belongs to you! Come!'

XXXI

MAJNUN, listening to his father, lowered
his eyes and remained silent. For some
days he obeyed his father's wishes. He rested, ate and
drank, dressed like other people, gave up composing
poetry and listened quietly when his father talked of
their homeward journey together. Did he succeed in
deceiving him? He wanted to with all his heart, not
only now but for all the days and nights still granted
to the old man on earth. But that was beyond his
strength. Unable to lie, even from pity, regret or
shame, he at last said to his father:

'You are my soul's life-giving breath. I am the
obedient slave of your counsels, which enlighten my

being, unravelling all knots. I have done everything to obey you, and know that I should follow your advice. Yet I cannot, my father! It is my fault! You strike your coins with the die of wisdom, mine is the die of love; it cannot be changed! Can you not see that I have forgotten my past? My memory is blank, the gale has blown away all I possessed....I am no longer the man I was, my father! If you ask me what happened, I cannot tell you, I don't remember. I know that you are my father and that I am your child. But I have even forgotten your name, I don't remember.'

In this hour Majnun understood his fate, and exclaimed:

'I have not only lost you; I no longer know myself. Who am I? I keep turning upon myself, asking "What is your name? Are you in love? With whom? Or are you loved? By whom?..." A flame burns in my heart, a flame beyond measure, which has turned my being to ashes. Do I still know where I live? Do I still taste what I eat? I am lost in my own wilderness! I have become a savage with wild beasts as my companions. Do not try to bring me back to the world of humans! Believe me, I am a stranger to them. One must not keep a melon in the garden once it has been poisoned by a fly, lest it infect the others. I am drawn towards death—death is within me. If only you could forget that you ever had a son! If only you could erase me from the book of those born into the world. If only

you could bury me here and think: Some fool, some
drunken madman....What was to be expected of him?
...Oh my father! You say that soon you will have to
begin your last journey? You say, this was the reason
why you came to fetch me? But it is late, too late for
both of us. It is autumn, here and inside me, and I
must depart—perhaps even before you. Let the dead
not mourn the dead, my father.'

XXXII

L ISTENING to these words, the father
understood that Majnun was his no longer.
He was a prisoner in the land of love, and no one
could bring him back.

'O you, my dearest,' replied the Sayyid, taking
Majnun in his arms, 'you consume yourself in your
grief, feeding on your own liver. You are my yoke,
but also my crown....Let me then take leave of us
both, of you and of myself. Look, our tears mingle
and flow together; they will cleanse me, and in the
cradle which is being prepared for my journey I shall
have wonderful dreams. Hold me fast. This hour will
have to nourish me on my way; it must last for a long
time. I too have tied my bundle in this world. Don't
you feel that I am not so far from your own? I fade
away, and your sufferings become mine. Never again
will I set eyes on you. Farewell. The boat which is

waiting for me will not return. Farewell! Where I am going, men wait for the resurrection. Farewell! I feel as if I had already been taken out of myself. Are we not both late? Is not our caravan on its way? Farewell, farewell; never in this world shall we meet again. '

The old man had spoken the truth. He reached home, but soon afterwards his strength failed, and his soul unfolded its wings. For two days it hovered, then, breaking its fetters, the heavenly bird took flight and found its resting place at the throne of Truth, while the earth received what belonged to her.

He who remains a stranger in this world and wanders, restless as the moon at night, will find peace. Man is as lightning, born to die, not to seek permanence in the house of suffering. Do not settle down to rest here, where everything perishes; you will only regret it later. But if you die your own death in this life, tearing yourself away from the world which is a demon with the face of an angel, you will share eternal life. You are your fate; your death, your life. Good will be joined to good, evil to evil. The echo shouts your secret from the mountain-tops, revealing only what you confided yourself.

XXXIII

I T happened during these days that a hunter of the tribe of Amir was stalking deer in the desert of Najd. One evening they met. Majnun was not the hunter's prey, but his tongue was as sharp as his sword.

'Have I to find you here,' he shouted, 'far away from your people? Do you not know anyone now except Layla? Have you forgotten father and mother? You should be ashamed, shameless one! A son like you would be better beneath the ground than above it. True, you probably left your father alive, young fool; but now he is dead, may you live long yourself! Will you not think of him, even now? Go away, go! Your place is at his grave. Do not refuse this last sign of affection to the dead. Ask his soul to forgive you for all your sins while he was alive!'

His words hit Majnun like a blow. A deep moan was his only answer. His body writhed and bent, and he looked like a harp plucked by torturing fingers. Then he fell and his forehead struck the ground time and again.

When he recovered, he hurried day and night to his father's tomb. Again grief threw him unconscious to the ground. His father, unable to rescue him, had at least shared his suffering. Their tears had mingled, now his must fall alone. Scourged by pain, Majnun clawed the dust with his fingers and, weeping, beseeched his dead father for some response, however slight.

'Father, oh father,' he implored, 'where are you?

Where do I find you, who have looked after me and suffered so much for my sake? Now you are no longer here, to whom can I talk? How happy you would have been if only I had been a better son to you! I have pushed you into the grave where now you lie buried....Oh father, how bitter it is to have lost you! I never knew, and now that I have learnt, it is too late. How grievous to be separated from you! You were my companion, my protector, the pillar of my strength; you were my master, you understood my sufferings and bore them with me! What am I now, alone and without you? Why did I remain when you left? Do not reproach me for my failure. I am nothing before you but shame!'

Full of sorrow and regret, Majnun exclaimed:

'I know that you wanted only my good. I rejected your helping hand. You were gentle, I was hard; you offered me warmth, I answered coldly. You suffered a thousand times, yet I did not come; you prepared a bed for me and I refused; you offered me a banquet, and I felled the tree you had planted, without tasting its fruit....All this I know, my father. Nothing is left to me but unending pain and countless regrets. You created a home for me in a corner of your heart: now that the arrow of fate has robbed me of it, I am trying to reach it. How did this happen? I was at home with you; suddenly you have gone and I am still here? How great is my sin! But I understand: Mine is the guilt; mine be the grief!'

So Majnun lamented, tearing his heart asunder in wild desperation, until the black flag of the night was lowered about him and his despair. Only when a new day climbed the mountain-tops and the breath of the sun turned dust into gold, did Majnun leave his father's tomb, returning, like a fleeting shadow, to the caves and ravines of Najd.

XXXIV

AFTER his father's death, the wilderness became Majnun's only refuge. Restlessly he roamed through its gorges and climbed steep rocks which no human being had explored before. He appeared now here, now there, as if searching for hidden treasure, seemingly one with the rocks, like the wild basil clinging to them. But this shy human flower carried a deathly grief in its calyx. Its name was Layla; she was the treasure which he hunted, and his life was nothing but longing for her. Day and night this flame burned inside him. He had been driven from his home by his desperate desire to find a home with her. If, in the distance, he espied tents and camp fires, he was attracted like a night-moth, as if they were secret signs sent out by his beloved.

One day he came across a group of people, all of whom knew him, or at least had heard of him—who among the Arabs had not? They stared when suddenly he noticed at his feet a scrap of paper, tossing in the wind. It bore the names 'Layla' and 'Majnun' written by an unknown hand, in tribute to their loyalty. Nothing else; just the two names joined together. Majnun snatched up the paper, peered at it then tore it in two; screwing up the part bearing the word 'Layla', he threw it carelessly away, keeping the other half with his own name.

The people looking on were greatly astonished, they would have expected anything but this. Surrounding the poet, they questioned him excitedly:

'What does this mean? Tell us, why have you done this? Here, you were united, and now you have separated yourself from her. Why?'

'Because,' said Majnun, 'one name is better than two. One is enough for both. If you knew what it means to be a lover, you would realize that one only has to scratch him, and out falls his beloved.'

But they were still not satisfied.

'Very well,' they said, 'one name is enough for both, that is what you say. Maybe! But why, then, do you throw away Layla and keep yourself? Why not the other way round?'

'Because one can see the shell, but not the kernel,' said Majnun. 'Do you not understand? The name is only the outer shell and I am this shell, I am the veil. The face underneath is hers.'

XXXV

THUS he spoke, and continued on his way, leaving behind the people and their tents. Love was glowing in him. When it burst into flames it also took hold of his tongue, the words streaming unbidden from his lips, verses strung together like pearls in a necklace. Carelessly he cast them away as toys for the wind to play with. What did it matter to the poet? Was he not rich? Was he not free? Had he not severed the rope which keeps men tied together? To his own kind he had become a savage, but even a savage is not entirely alone in this world, even a Majnun has companions. His were the animals.

He had come as a stranger into their realm, yet had not hunted them. He had crept into their caves without driving them out. Just as they, he was afraid and fled whenever men approached. Did Majnun, therefore, appear to the animals like an animal himself? Not entirely: they sensed that he was different. He possessed a strange power, unlike that of the lion, the panther or the wolf, because he did not catch and devour smaller animals. On the contrary, if he found one of them caught in a trap, he stroked its fur, talked until it had calmed down, and then released it. Why? What kind of a creature was he? Who could understand him? He fed on roots,

grass and fruit—but even of these he ate sparingly—and showed no fear of the powerful four-footed beasts of prey which could so easily have torn him to pieces and devoured him. Yet they did not do so. To everyone's surprise, Majnun was never threatened by any of the beasts that hunt in the steppe and the desert. They became used to his appearance; he even attracted them. Catching his scent from afar, they came flying, running, trotting, creeping, drawing narrowing circles around him. Among them were animals of every kind and size, but—what a miracle!—they did not attack each other, and lost all fear, as long as this trusted stranger stayed in their midst. They seemed to forget their hunger and became tame and friendly.

At last a lion began to keep watch over Majnun, like a dog guarding a flock. Other animals followed, a stag, a wolf, a desert fox. Every day there were more of them. If Majnun rested the place soon looked like an animal camp. He became a king among his court, like Solomon. Does one not think of a vulture as a bone-picker? And was not Majnun merely a skeleton covered with skin? Yet he rested peacefully in the shade of the vultures' wings, which at noon protected him against the heat of the sun. What a good king indeed! One who never oppressed his own subjects, nor extorted taxes, nor sacrificed their blood to make war on other peoples.

Guided by the vultures' example, the other beasts of

prey also lost their urge to kill. The wolf no longer devoured the lamb, the lion kept his claws off the wild ass, the lioness gave milk to the orphaned baby gazelle and the jackal buried his age-old feud with the hare. It was a peaceful army that travelled with Majnun as he roamed the wilderness, his animals always at his heels. Was their love less rewarding than that of human beings? Do not believe it.

If Majnun wanted to rest, the fox swept a place clean for him with its tail. The wild ass offered its neck as a pillow, the stag its loins as a bolster. The gazelle caressed his feet, the lion kept watch ready to pounce, and wolf and panther circled the camp as keen-eyed scouts.

Thus each animal assiduously did its duty, watching over Majnun, protecting and caring for him. He lived among all these creatures like an exiled ruler in a foreign country, or rather like an angel with his wings tied.

But the more be became the master and friend of the animals, the less often did he encounter human beings. Many of those who had visited him feared his new followers. When he appeared with his companions, people avoided him. If somebody insisted on seeing him, the animals, full of suspicion, gathered around their king, bared their teeth and growled, until Majnun calmed them down and ordered that the visitor be admitted. Then the stranger remained unharmed. If, however, he intended to disturb, harm or mock, he had to make good his escape speedily, lest sharp teeth and claws should tear his garments and his limbs. There was no longer admission to this chieftain without special permission.

Had anyone ever known a shepherd like Majnun? Was there ever a shepherd with such a flock? Leaving the human world, he had come to the wilderness reconciling wild ones with wild ones.

How surprised people were when this story reached the tents and, from there, the villages and towns. How was it possible? Was it not a fairy-tale, a saga from times gone by? Many just would not believe until they had seen with their own eyes. Some even undertook long journeys to satisfy their curiosity or their doubts. When they found Majnun surrounded by his court of loyal four-footed and winged followers, they did not know what to think or what to say, and their surprise was unbounded.

Many pitied him and brought food and drink, knowing that out of love for Layla, he had become a hermit. But Majnun accepted no more than a bite or a sip. Everything else he gave to his animals.

And as he was good, so they became good also.

XXXVI

ARE animals not an echo of human beings? They are what we make of them. I remember a story I was once told, of a ruler in the town of Marw. Listen! This king had a number of watch-dogs. They were not ordinary dogs, rather they resembled chained demons. Every one had the strength of a wild boar, and their massive jaws were strong enough to sever the head of a camel with one bite.

You will ask: 'Why did the king keep such monsters?' Well, there was a good reason. If someone fell out of favor with the king and aroused his wrath, he was thrown to these hounds, who would tear the victim to pieces and devour him.

Among the king's courtiers there happened to be a youth of great intelligence, well versed in all arts and devices. He knew, of course, all about the canine monsters and their terrifying purpose. However happy he appeared outside, secretly he trembled. Was not the king a moody hothead, wild and irascible? Was he not capable of hating tomorrow whom he loved today? And how quickly that could happen, in spite of all caution! A ruler's favor is as unpredictable as the sky in spring. The young man shuddered, thinking of the fate which might be in store for him. What was he to do?

After deep thought he made his decision. As if by chance, he began to walk in the neighborhood of the kennels and to exchange friendly words with the keepers whenever there was an opportunity. He also unobtrusively gave them small presents and so gradually won their confidence and good will.

When this first step had succeeded, he took the next. Friendship with the keepers opened the door to friendship with their charges. Now, he brought presents for the dogs, pieces of meat, sometimes a whole sheep. He began to humor these wild beasts and talk to them until they became more and more familiar and began to expect him, howling with pleasure and leaping up impatiently in their cages as soon as they saw him coming. He was now able to stroke them and pat their heads without danger; which had been his object from the beginning.

That is how things were when, on one unlucky day, the king, for no particular reason, became angry with the young courtier. In his blind fury he gave the order to throw the unhappy man into the kennels. The king's will was done. Tying the helpless youth hand and foot, the guards pushed him in front of the bloodthirsty beasts. But what did these monsters do? Human beings may be ungrateful; not so wild dogs! When they recognized their friend, who was unable to move, they gathered round him, wagging their tails and licking his face and hands lovingly to show their affection Then they crouched around him like sentinels, ready to defend him against his enemies and to protect him from danger. Nothing could tempt them away.

How surprised were the henchmen who had banked on watching from a safe distance a cruel and bloodthirsty spectacle. Instead, they witnessed an example of affection between man and animal. They could hardly believe their eyes, but the dogs simply disregarded their shouts.

What in the meantime happened to the king? When the day went to its rest, draping the gold-embroidered veil of the approaching twilight over its white garment, the monarch's wrath began to abate. As yet he did not know what we have already heard, because no one dared to tell him, but, regretting his rash order he felt deeply remorseful and finally said to his friends: 'Why ever did I let the dogs tear this innocent gazelle to pieces? Go and see what has happened to the poor man.'

The courtiers did as they were told, and returned with one of the guards, ordering him to report to the king. No one will be surprised to hear that this man was afraid to tell the whole truth and to confess how the youth, by showing friendliness and distributing presents, had won the confidence of the dogs and their guards. So he said: 'Your Majesty! This youth cannot be human, he must be an angel from heaven for whom the Almighty has worked a miracle. Come and see for yourself! There he sits, surrounded by all these hounds; not even baring their teeth, they nuzzle and lick him. Is that not clearly God's work? These dogs, as you know, are wolves with dragons' faces; yet, oh king, not one of them has harmed so much as a hair of his head!

When the king heard this, he jumped from his throne, rushing to the kennel as fast as his legs would carry him, to save the unhappy youth, if possible, in the nick of time.

But there was little need for haste. The king saw the miracle with his own eyes. Tears rolled down his cheeks like torrents, and when the guards had untied the condemned man and brought him out of the kennel, the king, sobbing violently, embraced him, asking his forgiveness a thousand times.

The king, however, did not altogether believe in miracles. After a while his curiosity was aroused and when he was alone with the rescued man, he asked: 'Now tell me how this really happened? How did you remain unharmed in there, even for one minute?'

The youth was too clever to hide the truth from the king; having told him the whole story, he continued:

'You see, your dogs became fond of me and saved my life for a few chunks of meat. And you, my king? You know quite well that I have served you loyally ever since I was a boy—for ten long years! Yet, just because I once annoyed you, you intended to destroy me, and wanted your hounds to tear me to pieces. Who, then, is a better friend, you or your dogs? Who deserves confidence and respect, you or the dogs?'

Thus he spoke, with great daring. But this time the king was not angry. He accepted this experience as a sign and a lesson, however bitter the dose. In future he left the dogs to themselves and no longer threw men into their cage to be devoured; instead he tamed the beast in his own soul.

But let us return to Majnun. He was kind to the animals, not from fear, but out of the goodness of his heart, and they remained loyal to him, just as the dogs were loyal to the youth of Marw. As we shall see, they stayed with him to the last, even longer. Although free and wild, they followed him wherever he went and rested wherever he did.

Do you grasp the significance? Do you understand the meaning? If you, too, follow Majnun, you will not have to drink the bloodstained water of this perishable world.

XXXVII

THE night was as light as day, and the face of the sky a garden of flowers, hung resplendent high above the earth. Sparkling like a golden ornament, the firmament kept turning. The seven planets, their hands linked, trod out the dance of fate on the carpet of the horizon. Meteors hurtled through the dome of heaven like spears of light thrown against demons. The air was impregnated with scent and the jewel of the moon was spreading a garment of silver rays over mountains and valleys Truly, the royal tent of this night was a matchless miracle, full of wonders.

Like a great shah, the full moon was riding through it, draped in golden brocade. Mercury was his arrow, shot from the royal bow. Venus, the dancer, adorned the border of his saddle as a lovely ornament, while the sword of the sun which during the day scorches the world, remained hidden in its scabbard. In the heat of anger, Mars was seeking to blind the eye of his enemy, while Jupiter carried the salvation of the world in his sleeve. Hanging from Saturn's belt was the steel rod which he uses secretly in the darkness to sharpen the sword of the morning.

But it was still night. Lonely, Majnun stood under the sky, his eyes wandering from star to star. Which of them would come to his aid? At last, during this journey, his eye reached Venus, and it was she whom the lover addressed first.

'Venus, lighting up the night, beacon for all those who are searching for happiness in the world. Mistress of singers and dancers. Your hand holds the key to success, your wine sparkles in every goblet. You are the seal in the king's signet ring, the queen in the palace of prosperity, the star of noble men and intimate friends. Your gift is the pleasantry on sensitive lips and those who belong to your circle are scented with ambergris. Be gracious also to me. Open for me the gates of hope, do not let me wait and starve outside. Look! My soul is sick and who but you would know the cure? Let me inhale the scent of my beloved while there is still time.'

After his prayer to Venus, Majnun's eye wandered along the seam of the sky until he encountered Jupiter. Could he not also help? Majnun addressed these words to him:

'Jupiter, star of delight! Whatever you promise, you keep your word. Yours is the care of our souls. You put your imprint on each kingdom in the world, for you are the star of just rulers and judges. It is you who writes the Book of Grace and you who determines who is to be victor and conqueror. The structure of the world rests on you. You give my fate its grandeur, my heart draws its strength from you. Keep faith with me! Do not turn your eye away, help me—help me, if there is still help for me.'

XXXVIII

THUS Majnun, in the darkness of night, cried out to the stars from the depths of his tortured heart; but there was no response. The heavens remained silent and the human soul froze in the ice-cold glow of the stars. Seeing them go on their way unconcerned, he suddenly understood. They could not show him the way out of his despair. They were blind and deaf, their glittering splendor was mute. What did human agony mean to the stars?

Yet he raised his voice for the third time. Where there are ruled, there is a ruler. He who is not heard by creation, may be heard by the creator, and so Majnun prayed to him who has created everything on earth and is without need:

'Where is my refuge, if not with you? Venus and Jupiter are your slaves and your name is the well-spring of all names. Your knowledge towers above all knowledge and your bounty is beyond all price. There is no chain which you could not break. You are the judge, the Lord of all Being. The deeds of the great ones of the world are your deeds and you come to the help of those who need you in their misery. We are all prisoners in chains, every one of us, and there is no help for those whom you do not help, O God. The seven heavens and all they may contain, lie at your feet. All things great and small, high and low, obey every gesture of your hand. The eye which saw you would be extingrushed in yours for eternity. The soul of him who is your dog, remains pure; woe to those who are not with you, but against you! I was earth, dark and heavy; your grace has changed me into pure water. So I am dead to myself. Do not let me lose my way and perish, do not exclude me from your charity; only your grace can change my darkness to light and lift me out of the black night of my fate into your eternal day.'

When Majnun had ended his prayer, a deep calm overcame him. His eye no longer roamed over the night sky. His heart felt at home and when sleep gently touched his shoulder, he did not notice it. He had a strange dream:

A tree grew out of the ground in front of him; quickly it reached great height and extended its crown towards the centre of the sky. Following its growth with his eyes, Majnun suddenly noticed a bird fluttering fearlessly through the leaves towards him from the farthest branch. Something glittered in its beak, like a drop of light. Just over Majnun's head, the bird let it drop. It was a jewel, which fell on to the crown of Majnun's head and remained lying there, a shining diadem.

The sleeper awoke. Already the roseate fingers of the new day had touched the seam of the horizon. The treasured dream vanished. Still, Majnun's whole being was flooded by a feeling of happiness such as he had not experienced for a long time. Did the bird of his soul take wing? Did not his body feel light, as if it could fly? Thus a dream may bring fulfilment at night to those who must live out their days without love.

XXXIX

SOMETIMES a dream's reflected radiance, enlightens our day. That is what happened to Majnun. It was a day which made every eye shine brighter, one of those mornings which waft a scent of paradise over the world, as if its breeze were the breath of the Messiah awakening the dead. How could the seed of misfortune prosper in such an hour?

Fate itself had grown tired of abuse. It had sent out happiness, but was it not too late? Let us see.

Majnun was sitting in one of his retreats on a mountain slope, protected by rocks, and, as always, surrounded by his animals. Suddenly he noticed in the far distance at the bottom of the valley a small cloud of dust. Violet-colored, it whirled into the silver light of the morning. The small cloud came nearer. It looked like a veil over a woman's face, and just as one can sometimes picture the face hidden beneath it, Majnun perceived a rider in the haze.

What did he want here, what was he looking for, all alone, when near or far there was no tent, no path? Perhaps he was looking for him, Majnun? But the face and figure of the rider were unfamiliar. Now the man, still far away, jumped from the saddle and continued his way up the mountain on foot. He proceeded slowly, carefully and with difficulty, for he was old. Or was he afraid of the court surrounding the king of the wilderness? Was he an enemy? Majnun was reminded of the black camel-rider who once brought him the ill-fated tidings of Layla's marriage.

But there was no resemblance to that fearsome messenger. The old man's face was noble and dignified. By now, the animals had become restive, warning the stranger. A slight growl became audible here, a snarl there, there was a scratching of the ground, a tapping, a stealing forward. But Majnun lifted his hand and at once all became quiet. Then he rose, advanced towards the unknown visitor and when he reached him, spoke kindly to him:

'Shining star, where does your journey take you? You and I—we do not know each other. Tell me, what good do you bring me? I like your face; but look, my animals there do not trust you…neither should I. Who has once been bitten by a serpent will be afraid, thereafter, even of an innocent coil of rope, and I, you must know, have been bitten not by a serpent, but by a veritable dragon! Some time ago another rider came to me and drove a thorn right into my heart; its point still lodges inside and causes pain. If, therefore, you have come to do the same as he, you had better keep silent and retrace your steps.'

The stranger, hearing these words, threw himself at Majnun's feet like a shadow and replied:

'Noblest among noble creatures! You have made the beasts of the wilderness your companions. Gazelles give you their love, and you stroke lions as if they were house-cats. You and yours need not be afraid of me. I am not your enemy, but a friend carrying a message from your beloved! A secret message, tidings such as no one has brought before: from her—to you alone. Now you know! With your permission I shall talk, but if you prefer me to remain silent, I shall return the way I came.'

Such words Majnun had not expected! His heart began to dance in feverish hope, and he exclaimed:

'If it is so—speak! Speak quickly!'

'I know,' the old man began, 'that your horoscope has behaved like an obstinate horse, trying to throw its rider, but why should it not be possible to tame it? To begin, let me tell you what has happened to me. Only a few days ago I passed a tented camp and close by was a garden—a grove with water, flowers and palm trees. As I let my eyes roam about, what did I see but someone sitting there alone, nearly hidden amongst the leaves. Someone? Well, let me tell you: I thought I was looking through the trees at a veiled star which had just dropped from the sky, a moon, a sun! I can only say that *she* was sitting there in this garden as if she herself were part of the Garden of Paradise. Because you must know that it was *she*. A little stream ran through the oasis, but when this girl, with eyes like a gazelle, began to talk, the words emerged from the well-spring of her lips so sweetly that all the other rippling waters ceased to murmur and to splash, listening to her dreamily. And her eyes! Even your lion would fall asleep like a hare once the eyes of this gazelle fell on him from behind her veil. All the beauties of our written characters are united in her: her hair is waved like the letter "Jim", slender and lithe like an "Alif" is her figure, and her mouth is curved like a "Mim". Adding these three letters

together, you get the word "Jam", which means "goblet" and that is what she really represents: a miraculous goblet, whose mirror reflects the secret of the world.

Her eyes are narcissi, flowering at the mouth of a spring and when you look into their calyxes you can see her wondrous dreams....But what am I saying? Her beauty blossoms like light radiating from the eye, like life-giving breath; but it is marred by suffering and weakness, which have bent her figure. Pearls of sorrow glint in the corners of her eyes, and the swaying reed has become a flute of sadness; the purple is muted to palest gold.'

After this attempt to describe Layla's appearance, he

continued:

'Believe me, all her hopes are concentrated on you, and fear alone induced her to marry. I saw her weeping, and it was as if a veil of moonlight enveloped the sun. How piteous a sight! I approached her and asked: "Who are you? And why so sad? For whom are you weeping?"

'She lifted her face, her sweet lips smiling with grief, and replied: "Why do you pour salt into my wounds? Let me tell you that once I was Layla, now I am Layla no longer. I am madder, more 'Majnun' than a thousand Majnuns. Is not Majnun the black star, a vagrant tormented by love? But my torments are a thousand times greater! It is true, he also is a target for the arrows of pain, but he is a man, I am a woman! He is free and can escape. He need not be afraid, can go where he likes, talk and cry and express the deepest feelings in his poem. But I? I am a prisoner.

'"I have no one to whom I can talk, no one to whom I can open my heart: shame and dishonor would be my fate. Sweetness turns to poison in my mouth. Who knows my secret sufferings? I cover the abyss of my hell with dry grass to keep it hidden. I am burning day and night between two fires.

'"Now—love cries out in my heart: 'Get up! Flee, like a partridge, from this raven father, this vulture husband.'

'"Now—reason admonishes me: 'Beware of disgrace! Remember—a partridge is not a falcon! Submit and bear your burden!'

'"Oh! A woman may conquer a hero and enslave him so that he lies prostrate at her feet; still she remains a woman, unable to act. She may thirst for blood and show the courage of a lioness—still she remains tied to woman's nature. As I cannot end my suffering, nothing is left for me but to yield. I am not allowed to be with Majnun, but I hunger for news of him: how does he spend his days, where does he stay? What does he do as he roams the desert? Has he any companions? Who are they? What does he say, what does he think? If you know anything about him, stranger, tell me, I implore you!"

'These were Layla's own words. And I? Well, I see you today for the first time face to face, but already I know much about you. I have not grown old and seen the world for nothing. Do not people everywhere tell of you and your love? Who is better known among the Arabs? How strange! Everyone knows; Layla alone is not allowed to hear! Is that fair? That is why I stayed for a while and talked to her of you. My words left an impression on her heart, like a seal in wax.

'"Majnun lives alone," I told her, "without family or friends, like a hermit, wrapt in memories of his love. His only companions—so I have heard—are animals which shun men, antelopes, wild asses and others.

But a love like his is too strong for man's weak nature. Suffering has broken him and his mind has become sick. Then his father died and this new blow bent him even lower. Thus fate strews his path with thorns day after day, and he has become the poet of his own misfortune. His verses tell the story of his grief and his love, and tears stream from his eyes like a thousand torrents; often he laments his dead father in words which would draw tears from a black stone."

'Thus I spoke, reciting some of your lines which I know by heart. She gave a deep sigh, and trembled; her head drooped as if she were about to die, far from you. She wept for a long time, lamenting your father's memory, saddened because you were now doubly alone and she could not be with you to share your grief....Then suddenly decision came to her. Pointing out her tent in the distance, she said:

'"Your mind is noble and your heart is pure. I trust you. Swear that you will return tomorrow. In the meantime, down there in my tent, I shall write a letter to Majnun and hand it to you. Then I want you to search until you find him! Will you?"

'I promised, and so we met again the next day. In honor of your father she wore a dark-blue dress, a mourning robe. In its folds she had hidden a sealed letter. She gave it to me. Here it is!'

The old man took a letter from his bag, kissed it and

handed it to Majnun. Could he know how much this meant to the lover? At first there was no sign. Majnun stood as if dreaming with open eyes. Without a word he kept staring at his hands, which held the sealed message. Was it too much for him? Had it come too suddenly? Did he not understand? Was it more than he could bear? Was it not a gift more precious to him than all the treasures of the world?

Suddenly a demon seemed to seize his rigid figure. Like a raving madman he tore the rags from his body. Then he began to dance, ever faster, ever wilder. He leapt high into the air, turning like a whirling top. Again and again, hundreds of times.

He did not stop until he collapsed. Unconscious, he lay on the ground, motionless as the stones around him, like a man whom wine has driven to raving madness and then cut down, robbed of his senses. But his fingers still gripped the paper tightly and when he came to, his first glance was at the letter. His heart was beating more calmly and he broke the seal.

XL

LAYLA had written:

'I begin this letter in the name of a king, who gives life to the soul and refuge to wisdom. He is wiser than all wise men, and he understands the language of those who cannot speak. It is he who has divided the world into light and darkness, and who gives its span of life to every creature, from the bird in the sky to the fish in the depths of the sea. He has adorned the heavens with stars and filled the earth with people. His majesty is without beginning or end. He has given them a soul, has lit it with the torch of reason and then illumined the world for both.'

Then she continued:

'This message is like a brocade sent by a griefstricken woman to a man of sorrows. It comes from me, a prisoner, and is meant for you, who have broken your chains. How long ago, my love, did I seal my bond with you! How fare you? What fills your days, you to whom the seven planets, these heavenly cradles, show the way? I know that you are guarding the treasure of friendship, and love derives its splendor from you. I see that your blood colors the mountains red at dawn and at dusk, but you live hidden deep down in the rocks like agate. In the midst of darkness you are the well-spring of Khizr, whence gushes forth the water of life. You are the night-moth, encircling the candlelight of an eternal morning. You have stirred up the world, yet turned your back towards it, living in the tomb of your loneliness, where only two or three wild asses are your companions. Here on earth you are a target for the arrows of reproach, but what is that to you? Is not your caravan on its way towards the day of resurrection?

'I know that you have not spared yourself, that you threw fire into your own harvest. You dedicated your heart to my service, and so became the target for slander. What matters it to you, what to me? We remain loyal to each other. If I only knew what you are feeling, how you look and what you are doing. With all my love I am with you and you are, tell me—with whom? Like your happiness, I am separated from you; but even if remote from you, I remain your companion.

'True, I have a husband! A husband, but not a lover; for he has never shared my bed. Believe me, the days have exhausted me, but no one has yet touched the diamond; the treasure of love has remained sealed, like the bud of an enchanted flower which will never open. My husband waits helplessly before my closed door.

'Even though he has dignity and fame—what does that mean to me? Who is he compared with you, my beloved? Seen from afar even garlic looks like a lily. But if you smell it, where is the lily's scent? It is not worth gathering. A cucumber may remind you of a pomegranate. But taste it, and you will know that it was only the shape and not the flesh.

'Oh my love! How I wish we could build our nest together in this world! But we may not. It is denied us. Is that my fault? My heart, which cannot make you happy, weeps over our sad fate.

'Beloved! Send me a hair of your head, and it will mean the world to me. Send me one of the thorns lying in your path, and it will blossom into a rose-garden before my eyes....Where your foot touches it, my Khizr, my messenger from God, the desert breaks into blossom; be my water of eternal life! I am the moon which looks at you from afar, to receive your light, my sun. Pardon my feet for being so weak that they can never reach you.

'I heard of your father's death, and rent my robe from top to bottom. In sorrow, I beat my face with my hands as if my own father had died. As a sign of mourning I dressed in dark blue, like a violet, and my eyes, full of tears, are like the calyx of a blossom blinded by golden dust. Do you understand me, my love?

'I have done everything to share your grief; everything, except this: I did not come to you myself; that was impossible. What matter? Our bodies are separated, but my soul is not divided from yours for a moment. I know what suffering is yours and how much your heart tortures itself. Yet there is only one way out of this despair for both of us; patience.

'Patience and hope. What is life in this world? It is only the tumult in an inn where we stop for a short rest. How quickly the days pass between arrival and departure! A wise man does not let others look through his eyes into his soul. Shall the enemy laugh at our tears? No! A wise man hides his grief lest the wicked and malicious should grow fat on such a feast.

'Do not look at the sower casting seed, but remember what will grow from it. If today thorns block your way, tomorrow you will harvest dates, and the bud still closed and hidden holds the promise of a blossoming rose.

'Do not be sad! Do not let your heart become heavy and do not think that no one is your friend. Am I no one? Does it not help you that I am there and am yours—yours alone? Believe me, it is wrong to complain of loneliness. Remember God. He is the companion of those who have no other friend.

'Even in your grief about your father you should not burst into flame or flash like lightning in the sky; do not drown in your tears like a rain-cloud. The father has gone, may the son remain! The rock splits and crumbles, but the jewel which it enclosed endures.'

Reading her letter and devouring every word with his eyes like a man starving, so great was his joy that he was quite beyond himself, like a bud bursting its sheath. For a long time he was unable to say anything but 'O God, my God...' and again 'O God.'

When he had partly regained his composure, his tears began to gush forth like a stream. He wept and wept while the messenger watched. Majnun seized the hands which had brought him the letter, covering them with kisses in wild gratitude, then prostrated himself before the old man, and kissed his feet. When he returned to his senses, what was his first thought? 'I want to answer Layla,' he said, 'now, immediately! I must....' But how? The poet whose pearls were offered in all the tents and bazaars of Arabia, had never written down his verses!

'How can I answer her?' he asked. 'I have neither paper nor pen.'

But the messenger smiled. As if he had thought this out a long time ago, he took a little case from his traveling bag, opened it and—behold! there, in beautiful order, were all the things needed by a writer. 'Here,' he said, 'help yourself!'

Majnun, without a second bidding, crouched on the ground, resting the paper on his knees, and wrote—or rather, painted—with tender care sign after sign. He did not need to think out what to say. How long had they grown in his heart, his love and his pain! Now he brought them out from the depths like a diver, spreading the precious stones before himself in the light of day, and stringing them together to a necklace of letters, of words, of points and curves and flourishes. Stone by stone he thus composed an image of his grief.

Then he handed the letter to the old man who, knowing how impatient the two lovers were, swiftly mounted his horse and sped away like the wind. He returned to Layla whose beautiful eyes read through a veil of tears what her lover had written to her in the wilderness.

XLI

MAJNUN'S letter also began with the evocation of God:

'You know everything which lies open to the light of day, but you also know what is hidden, for you have created both the rock and the precious stone within it. Yours is the firmament with all the constellations. You change the darkness of night into the light of day, and the hidden chambers of the human heart lie open to your eyes. You cause the sap to rise in the joyous days ot spring and lend a willing ear to the prayer of the unhappy man longing for consolation.'

Then Majnun addressed Layla:

'Having lost everything which binds me to this earth, I am writing this letter to you who hold my fate in your hands, and would be welcome to sell my blood as cheaply as you wish.

'You say that I am the keeper of the treasure? I am so close to it, yet so far! My key has not yet been made, the iron from which it is to be forged still sleeps in the rock.

'I am the trampled dust at your feet. You are the water of life—for whom? Prostrate, I lie beneath the soles of your feet and your arm embraces—whom? I would even suffer harm from you, while you are soothing—whose grief? I am your slave carrying on my shoulders your saddle-cloth—and you? Whose ring adorns your ear? You, my Kaaba with the beautiful face, you, my altar: you have become a threshold—for whom?

'You are my salve for a hundred thousand wounds, yet you are also my sickness and the wine in my beaker which does not belong to me. You are my crown which does not adorn my brow. Yes, you are my treasure enjoyed by a stranger, while I am but the beggar bitten by the serpent which guards you.

'You, my garden of paradise! Nowhere can I find a key to open the gate. My heavenly bosquet, how inaccessible you remain! From your forest comes the tree of my being. This tree is yours, and if you cut it down a part of yourself will die. I am the earth which you tread. If you caress me, I am the spring which bids flowers grow for you. But if you beat me, I am but the whirling dust which envelops you.

'Did I not lay my head willingly at your feet? Am I not famous as your slave? Be it so, I carry a burden befitting a slave. Be my Mistress and act your part. Where is my shield? I have thrown it away and surrendered to you. I have become your prisoner without a fight, but if you now refuse me, I shall be put to the sword.

'Show mercy to me and to yourself. Do not stone your own tool, do not fight your own army, do not sting your own body! Be gentle and mild, giving solace to my heart; thus slaves are set free.

'Does a knight desert his page? How could the page obey a master whom he never sees? Let me remain your slave! Do not barter me.

'Yet, have you not done so already? Did you not engrave my name in a sheet of ice which melts in the sun? Did you not lead me into the fire to be burned? Is not that what you did to me?

'Ah yes! You have changed my day into black night and have beaten me even though lamenting over it! That is not fair; to rob my heart, to abduct my soul and to think of me—when?

'You only sell me words which hurt, while I am burned to ashes by my love. And you? You, my dearest, who bought me: can I read in your face the signs of love? Show me where they are!

'Is that perhaps why you broke our tie, sealing a new bond with another? Is that so? You seduced me by words and gave him what love desires? Are your sighs sincere? And if not? Then your rule is tyranny.

'Do not be heartless: You share my grief. My eyes search only for you and, looking for the signs which herald my fate, I think only of you. Where can I find peace? He only is calm who is allowed to look at you, not he whose days pass like mine. He who possesses a jewel like you, also possesses vigor and joy.

'Alas, I do not possess you. Has that not always happened since the beginning of time? We dig for treasure, and the ground refuses to surrender it. Or, look at a garden! While the nightingale sings its praises, the raven devours its figs. And the pomegranate which the gardener nourished with the blood of his heart, is given away—who knows?—to sustain a sick fool. Fate has strange ways!

'When, oh my rose-colored ruby, when will you be freed from this millstone of a husband? Oh, moon who lights up my eyes, when will you escape from the jaws of this dragon? When will the bee take off and leave its honey to me? When will the mirror become free of rust? When will the door of the treasure-house open and the serpent which guards it die? When! When will the Mistress of the castle let me in?

'Yet, I do not bear hatred towards your husband. Though I have to live far from you in darkness and he is the moth fluttering around the lamp—may he enjoy the light, may he be happy!

'You are everything to me: good and bad, my sickness and my cure.

'Forgive me! Forgive me if I have suspected you, although I know that no one has yet stormed your fortress, that the shell guards your pearl and that in the hiding place of your hair no one has touched your treasure. I know, yes I know!

'But you also know the force of passion: jealous hearts can harbour evil thoughts. You know how much I am longing to be near you, and that I envy a hundred times the mosquito resting on you for a moment.

'What lover would be so blind that his eye and heart could not transform an insect into a vulture? Then the fever grips me and I feel that, like an ant, I cannot rest until I have driven that mosquito from the sugar. That mosquito? He is a noble man, Ibn Salam, your husband! I know that! But does it help me? For me, he is but a thief who enjoys what he has not paid for. One who worries about a rose which it is not his right to gather. One who guards a pearl which he never bought.

'Oh, my love, with your breasts like jasmin! Loving you, my life fades, my lips wither, my eyes are full of tears. You cannot imagine how much I am "Majnun". For you, I have lost myself.

'But that path can only be taken by those who forget themselves. In love, the faithful have to pay with the blood of their hearts; otherwise their love is not worth a grain of rye. So you are leading me, revealing the true faith of love, even if your faith should remain hidden from me forever.

'Let my love for you be the guardian of my secrets. Let the grief which this love causes me, be my soul's caress! What matters it that there is no healing salve for my wound? As long as *you* are not wounded, all suffering is nothing.'

XLII

AMONG Majnun's relatives there was one whose noble heart and keen mind had won the esteem of his fellow men. His name was Salim Amiri, and Majnun's mother was his sister. All who knew him thought highly of him, yet modesty remained the mark of his dignity.

This worthy man had always loved his nephew and dearly wanted to help him. But even he, who usually found a way out of every impasse and knew the cure for many an evil, had failed. Thus he had shared the younger man's sufferings only from afar, but as often as possible had sent presents of clothes and food to ease the hermit's misery. Now, however, the time seemed ripe to visit the lost one. Who knows, perhaps there was still a way to lead the estranged youth back to his home? But first he must trace the wanderer's steps, leading far away from the world of men.

So Salim mounted his strongest and fastest camel and set off. Caravans and inns became less and less frequent as he went, but that did not deter the courageous rider. Like a mad demon wind, he raced from desert to desert, never ceasing to search until in the end he discovered the fugitive in wild mountains where no human foot had penetrated before.

But this hermit was not alone. Salim found his nephew amidst a horde of wild animals. Had he assembled all the inhabitants of desert and steppe into a single army? When the rider faced their camp, fear crept up his spine. He stopped, waved to Majnun and shouted a greeting.

'Who are you, and what do you want?' came the answer.

'I am Salim, from the tribe of Amir,' was the reply, 'and I, too, am one with whom fate plays hazard on earth. But you should know that! I can see that the sun has changed you into a negro, but am I not still your uncle?'

Only then did Majnun recognize his visitor. He ordered his animals not to attack, received him with all honors and asked him to be seated. Then he enquired about kinsfolk and friends and his visitor's well-being. How surprised and happy was Salim to find his nephew so reasonable! Was this a madman, deserving of the name given to him? Of course, if one only judged by appearance the mistake was understandable. But as he examined his sister's son closely from head to foot, Salim felt shame and grief rise in his heart. How could this have happened?

Majnun walked like a corpse newly risen from the grave! Risen—where and for whom, for the beasts of the wilderness? A corpse would at least wear a shroud, while this man was stark naked.

No! A nobleman from the tribe of Amir must not expose himself like that, not even here in this man- and god-forsaken hideout, where only stars, rocks and animals could see him—that was intolerable.

Uncle Salim could stand the sight no longer. He took out his second garment and held it in front of Majnun: 'Forgive me! Would you mind putting this on? It is not decent that you should go naked; not, at least, while I am here.'

'Clothes are useless to me,' replied Majnun at once, 'my body is hot enough without them. It is a furnace in which a fierce flame is burning. As soon as I put on a garment, I tear it to shreds.'

But the uncle did not give in. He implored and insisted until Majnun complied with his wish. Then the guest produced all kinds of food from his bag, halwa, sugared bread and other delicacies. Who could have resisted? But the harder Salim pressed, the more stubborn Majnun became, refusing even to taste them. Instead, he gave the sweetmeats to his animals. And they liked them! When Salim realized that even his magic powers of persuasion were wasted and that the choicest sweets would only be thrown to the dogs, he asked:

'What do you feed on, then? If you are human, not a demon, you must eat, you unhappy creature. But what? What do you feed on?'

'My heart is "salim"—"sound"—like your name,' replied Majnun, 'even if my body has forgotten how to eat. All I can tell you is that I no longer desire food. A few roots and grasses are all I need. But I am not alone here. As you can see, my animals are only too happy to accept your presents. Watching them stills my hunger too.'

The uncle pondered these words for a little, then he said, smiling broadly:

'I understand, and perhaps you are right. After all, birds are caught in snares because they are greedy. Are human beings different? Our hunger is the snare in which fate catches us. The greedier we are, the greater the danger. Only he who, like you, is content with a little grass, is truly free; a king in his world. That brings to mind a story which you must hear.'

THE STORY OF THE SHAH
AND THE DERVISH

'Once upon a time a mighty king rode past the hut of a hermit. This pious man had turned away from the world, directing all his thoughts and desires towards the other life. His hut was a miserable hole with crumbling walls.

'The king was surprised. He could hardly believe that

anyone would want to live in such a hovel, and asked his retinue: "What does this man do here? What does he eat? Where does he rest his head? Who is he?"

'"He is a holy man," answered the king's followers, "well known not to require sleep or food. That distinguishes him from ordinary humans."

'The shah's curiosity was aroused. Reining in his horse and beckoning to his chamberlain, he approached the hermit. At some distance he stopped, waiting for his courtier to bring the holy man before him. The chamberlain advanced and said:

'"You, my man, have cut all ties with the world. You seem to be happy and content to live in this ruin. All alone? Why? Where do you find the strength to endure such misery? And what do you eat?"

'The holy man had just crushed some plants found in the steppe where the gazelles graze. He held them up and replied with equanimity:

'"This is what I eat! My ration for the journey."

'The spoiled courtier, supercilious as are those who serve kings, grimaced and asked contemptuously:

'"Why do you live in such misery? If you entered the service of our shah, you would have better food than grass!"

'"What do I hear?" asked the dervish indignantly. "You call this grass? My dear Sir, this isn't grass, these are honey blossoms! If you knew how good they taste, you would forget your shah and not remain in his service for another hour!"

'The king, too, heard these words and, being an intelligent man, realized their truth. Jumping from his horse and rushing up to the hermit he rendered homage to him and kissed him.

'And the king was right. Free is the man who has no desires.'

XLIII

MAJNUN liked Salim's story and listened with rapt attention. When his uncle had finished, Majnun appeared almost gay. He even laughed happily, jumped up, sat down again, and for a while vividly recalled the friends of his youth. He remembered them all and talked about them to Salim. Suddenly he thought of his mother. All gaiety faded from his face and he said, with tears in his voice:

'How is it that I have not thought of her for so long! Mother, my bird with the broken wings! Tell me quickly, how is she? Is she in good health, or has grief cut her down? I am her negro slave, my face blackened by shame. Yet how deeply I long to see her beauty!'

Here, too, Salim was able to give good counsel. He decided at once to fulfil Majnun's wish. Perhaps the mother could persuade her son to return to his home and tribe. This king of wild beasts—was he not human after all—and did he not belong among other humans?

'Be sure that I will bring your mother to you,' said Salim, when he took his leave. And he kept his promise, returning with her before many days had passed.

When the mother recognized her son from afar, her heart shrank. How the rose had faded, how clouded the mirror had become! She was not afraid of the animals; lion, panther and wolf—what concern were they of hers? She saw only her son in his unhappiness and rushed as quickly as her tired feet would carry her to embrace, kiss and caress her re-found child.

Is that not a mother's way always and everywhere? Without question, without demand, she simply follows the call of tenderness and pity.

She now washed in a flood of tears the poor face, so wasted, yet so familiar; now she tamed the wilderness of his hair with a comb taken from the folds of her dress. How neglected he was from head to foot. Moaning softly and caressing him, she tended the wounds caused by thorns and stones. When Majnun began at last to resemble the boy Qays, and when both had tasted the first pleasure and the first grief of their reunion, only then did the mother recover her speech:

'My son, what a robber you are. Is life for you nothing but a game of love? Your father has been felled by the sword of death, which is also threatening me—and you are still drunk with the wine of your youth! How much longer? Your father died in grief and sorrow and I am as good as dead, believe me. Come to your senses! Rise and return with me instead of despoiling your own nest. Take your example from the animals and birds of the wilderness. When night falls, they return to their nests and caves. Why not you? For how long will you hide from other men? For how long will you roam about without sleep or peace? Life is brief: it passes as quickly as two days. Prepare your bed and give yourself some peace. Why should you rest your head in caves? Why set your foot among ants and serpents? The serpent will bite you and, once you are dead, the ants will eat you anyway. So leave it at that. Stop torturing your soul. It is not a stone hardy enough to resist the force of the elements. Allow your soul its rest and your heart its peace! The heart also is no rock and you are not made of iron.'

Thus his mother beseeched him, and her words burned him with tongues of flame.

'Your foot be my crown,' he replied. 'I am the pearl which tortures the oyster. I realize that, yet there is no other course. Where is my fault, if I was given no choice? My life is in a desperate state but I have not chosen my fate voluntarily. What is the good of all our striving? Each must play his allotted part. You should know that I have never been free to accept or to refuse my love, permeated by so much suffering and misery. Therefore, mother, do not insist on my return! You want me to free the bird of my soul from its cage? But this cage is my love! I would never succeed. Even if I returned home I should only be caught in another trap, because what you call "home" is to me but a second prison, where—I fear—I would die, unless I escaped again. My home is my love; nowhere else am I at home. Leave me, therefore; do not press me. You, too, are unhappy because I suffer. I know that, yet I cannot help it; I cannot—forgive me!'

Majnun threw himself at his mother's feet as if he were her shadow; begging forgiveness, he kissed her feet, even the ground beneath them.

There was nothing the old woman could say or do. Weeping she took her leave and returned home with her brother Salim. But, longing for her child, home became foreign to her and before long she died, following her husband into the other world.

XLIV

ONCE more that royal horseman, the sun, galloped into the arena where the wheel of heaven turns. His rivals the stars went pale and retreated towards the rim of the horizon in the west. The shining rays of the conqueror made the crystal bowl of the night scintillate until the morning lifted it high and then broke it, so that the wine ran out, coloring the firmament purple from one end to the other. Thus day broke.

Majnun was sitting far from all human company, beating out on the drum of his loneliness qasid after qasid of his lovesongs; whether day or night mattered not to him. In his wilderness no one counted the hours. He did not know about the happenings in the world of men, great or small, not even that his mother had since left, departing farther than he himself had gone. He might never have learned it, had not his uncle, bringing food and clothes, visited him for the third time to tell him. Salim lifted his face up to the sun and lamented:

'In truth, your mother saw enough unhappiness in the light of her days. Now, far from you, she has closed her eyes. Tying her bundle, she has said farewell to the house of the world and has gone. You were missing when she left, but she was longing for you as your father before her.'

In deep distress Majnun battered his face with his fists. He wailed like a bewitched harp and struck the ground like glass hitting a stone. Then he raced away until he reached the place where his mother now lay beside his father.

He buried his face in the earth where the dead rest, waiting to be questioned by angels before the Last Judgment. His lament rose to the sky, but when has the wailing of man ever brought back the dead?

Those who heard him were the living. His family and the men of his tribe came rushing one after the other. Looking at Majnun, worn with misery and bowed by despair, they had to commiserate not only with his parents but also with himself, whether they liked it or not.

'We salute you,' they said, 'your grief is ours, and our home is yours. Stay with us, do not leave again!'

Whatever they said—Majnun's answer was but a moan. No—even now he was only a guest. Nothing, no one could hold him. His home was here no longer, his friends had become strangers. He tore himself away from their hands, his eyes leaping ahead of his steps into the mountains where only his animals awaited him; there was space for his heart to suffer from one rim of the sky to the other. For one brief moment he had hit the trail of men like a flash of lightning—then he vanished again like a cloud driven by the wind....

What is human life after all? Whether it endures for a brief spell or longer—even if it could last a thousand years; take it as a breath of air merging into eternity. From the beginning, life bears death's signature; they are brothers in the secret play of their eyes. For how long then do you want to deceive yourself? For how long will you refuse to see yourself as you are and as you will be? Each grain of sand takes its own length and breadth as the measure of the world; yet, beside a mountain range it is as nothing. You yourself are the grain of sand; you are your own prisoner. Break your cage, break free from yourself, free from humanity; learn that what you thought was real is not so in reality. Follow Nizami: burn but your own treasure, like a candle—then the world, your sovereign, will become your slave.

XLV

MAJNUN'S letter did not soothe Layla's grief; on the contrary, it increased her suffering and the sadness of her days. Majnun certainly only wanted to torture himself with his bitter laments and reproaches. But his heart knew the truth and at the end of his letter he admitted:

'Forgive! I suspected you, although I knew that no one had conquered your fortress....' Layla

understood her beloved and felt hurt only because he
hurt himself so deeply.

He in his wilderness could be as free and as mad as
he liked; *she* had always been a prisoner, first her
father's, then her husband's. A prisoner, courted,
loved and spoiled—but did that ease her fate? Her
husband obeyed, never touching her, but he lived in
hope and laid siege to her with his tenderness,
enclosing her in the walled city of his love. In jealous
loyalty he guarded the gate which he was not allowed
to enter.

But one night, which was as black as a Moor, Layla
managed to escape from the tent. She sensed that this
was not an ordinary night! Where was she to go? She
did not know; in the darkness she blindly followed a
voice in her heart which led her to the edge of a palm
grove where two paths crossed—the same place
where she had once met the old horseman who had
taken her letter to Majnun.

Who knows, suggested the voice, perhaps, as you
want it so badly, you will again receive word from
him here. And so it was!

When she reached the crossroads, she suddenly
perceived a shadow right in front if her. Like hers, his
steps seemed to be guided in the darkness by the
flaming torch of his heart. She knew at once that it
was the old man.

Who was he? Perhaps Khizr, God's messenger

himself? Layla did not ask; and as she had felt in her soul that she would meet him here, she was hardly surprised. She addressed him without hesitation: 'What news do you bring about the course of heaven? What does he do, my wild love in his wilderness? Of whom does he dream? What does he say?'

The old man did not seem surprised either, not by Layla, nor by her words. Gently he replied:

'Without you and your light, my moon, he about whom you enquire is like Joseph the youth at the bottom of the pit. His soul is like the ocean at night, whipped up by the gale under a moonless sky. Like a herald he roams through mountains and valleys shouting at every step; and what he shouts is "Layla", and what he seeks is Layla. Good or bad, he no longer knows himself. He is on his way to nowhere, for he has no goal left but—Layla.'

When the girl heard this, she became a reed sounding the melody of lost love. Her narcissus eyes overflowing with tears, she said:

'It is I who have burnt my lover's heart and brought this fate upon him! How I wish that I could be with him in his adversity! But our sufferings are not alike. It is I, not he, who is caught like Joseph in the pit. Majnun is free, walking over the mountain peaks where I cannot follow him out of my valley—yet I *will* see him!'

With these words Layla loosened some jewels from

her ear-rings, kissed them and handed them to the old man with these words:

'Accept these as a present; go, fetch Majnun and bring him here. Then arrange a secret meeting in this garden. I only want to see him, to look at him, one single glance into the light! How else can I know how he fares. How deep is his loyalty? And perhaps, who knows, he will recite a few of his lines for me, two or three only, which no one else has yet heard; perhaps when I listen to them the tangled skein in my soul will be unravelled.'

When he heard Layla's words the old man carefully tied the pierced pearls she had given him into his sash, then he took his leave of the matchless pearl whom no one had yet pierced.

He rode through the night and the desert while Layla's fears and hopes rode invisible beside him. Like a mariner sailing from island to island he traveled from oasis to oasis; but none of the Bedouin could put him on the track. Fate alone led him. He finally found the king of the wilderness at the foot of a mountain, surrounded by his animals, and as sad as a treasurer whose precious jewels are in the hands of a stranger.

Majnun was happy when he recognized the old man. Jumping up, he sharply ordered his growling and snarling companions to keep their peace. They calmed down, the messenger entered their circle and stopped in front of Majnun. Greeting him with the reverence due to a ruler, he bent down to the ground, invoked the grace of heaven on Majnun and spoke thus:

'Ruling in the realm of love, may your life endure as long as love itself. I am sent by Layla, whose beauty is one of the wonders of the world. She values her bond with you higher than her life. How long is it since she has seen your face, or heard your voice! She wishes to see you, so that eye can look into eye, if only for the passing of a breath. And you: would it not also make you happy to see her? Could you not once break the fetters of separation, recite verses which would bring peace to her heart, re-live what has become memory, re-awaken what belongs to the past?

'Look, I know of a garden where palm trees, as dense as a forest, will protect you from prying eyes. There will be nothing above but the wheeling expanse of the sky, nothing beneath but a carpet of living green....Come! Spring awaits you there and the key of your fate!'

With these words, the old man produced a garment from his bag and, with words of blessing, put it on Majnun who was almost numbed by what he heard. Was it really possible, then, to steal a glance at paradise while living on earth? Could a small particle of eternity break the chain of hours? How could this old man understand? What did people beyond the wilderness know about 'Majnun'? Their happiness was not his; there was fulfilment for their wishes, but not for his longing.

Yet, how could Majnun resist what was offered to him, how could he ignore the call of his beloved?

When the old man had dressed him fittingly for a journey into the world of men, they departed, followed, of course, by the caravan of animals who would not desert their shah wherever he went.

The nearer they approached Layla's abode, the more Majnun trembled in feverish desire. Impatience drove him on. It was as if a well-spring filled with the water of life was beckoning him from the horizon, as if the wind was even now wafting the scent of his beloved, as if he was dying of thirst while the waves of the Euphrates were receding from him....

But for once stubborn fate proved favorable to the lovers. One evening Majnun and his guide safely reached the palm grove where the animals were to camp and await their master's return. In the falling dusk Majnun himself went into the heart of the garden and sat down under a palm tree to rest, while the old man left, to give the pre-arranged signal to Layla.

The fairy girl, hidden in her tent, espied the old one at once from behind the curtain where she had waited so long, torn between fear, doubt and hope —though that was a small price to pay for the chance of seeing the beloved after years of separation.

Wrapped in her veil and protected by the growing darkness, Layla rushed to the garden, her soul flying ahead of her feet. She saw Majnun, but stopped before reaching the palm tree against which he was leaning. Her knees trembled and her feet seemed rooted in the earth beneath them. Only ten paces separated her from her beloved, but he was enveloped by a magic circle which she must not break. Turning to the old man at her side, she said:

'Noble sir! So far I am allowed to go, but no farther. Even now I am like a burning candle. If I approach the fire, I shall be consumed. Nearness brings disaster, lovers must shun it. Better to be ill, than afterwards to be ashamed of the cure....Why ask for more? Even Majnun, he, the ideal lover, does not ask for more. Go to him! Ask him to recite some verses to me. Let him speak, I shall be ear; let him be the cup-bearer, I shall drink the wine!'

The old man went, but when he approached the quiet figure under the palm tree, he saw that Majnun's head had sunk: he had fainted. Moved by pity and fear, the old man took the youth's head in his lap, showering the pallid face with tears. When Majnun came to, he drew himself up and, as his eyes found their way to Layla, the verses she had asked for began to flow from his lips.

XLVI

*A*nd who am I—so far from you, yet
near?
A singing beggar! Layla, do you hear?
Freed from life's drudgery, my loneliness,
Sorrow and grief for me spell happiness.
And thirsty in the painstream of delight,
I drown. Child of the sun, I starve at night.
Though parted our two loving souls combine,
For mine is all your own and yours is mine.
Two riddles to the world we represent,
One answer each the other's deep lament.
But if our parting severs us in two,
One radiant light envelops me and you,
*As from another world—though blocked and
barred*
What there is one, down here is forced apart.
Yet if despairing bodies separate,
Souls freely wander and communicate.
I'll live forever—Mortal Fear, Decay,
And Death himself have ceased to hold their
sway. Sharing your life in all eternity
I'll live if only you remain with me.

Layla listened while Majnun recited other poems.
Suddenly he fell silent, jumped up and fled from the
garden into the desert like a shadow. Though drunk

with the scent of wine, he still knew that we may taste it only in paradise.

XLVII

BY that time the caravans had brought Majnun's poems from the desert to the alleyways and bazaars of the towns. There lived a youth by the name of Salam in Baghdad on the Tigris. He was not lacking in beauty and intelligence, but had tasted love's sorrow. Being very fond of poetry, he soon learned of Majnun and of his love-songs for Layla. How miraculous!

I must find this Majnun, the youth thought, I must see him and talk with him, for he also is unhappy in love, and a famous poet....

No sooner thought than done. The youth tied his possessions into a bundle, mounted a camel and traveled to the country of the Bedouin.

For a long time he roamed the desert, searching and asking, until at last he found Majnun, naked from head to foot. When Majnun saw Salam and realized that he must have come from afar, he forbade his beasts to attack, then beckoned the youth to approach, greeted him kindly and asked:

'Where do you come from?'

'I have reached journey's end,' was the reply; 'my home is Baghdad and I have come for your sake into a strange land, to see your wondrous face and to hear your strange verses. As God has preserved my life, allow me to stay with you for a while. I want to be your slave, Enlightened One, to kiss the dust under your feet and to submit to your rule. Every verse you recite I will learn by heart, a vessel for your wine, a treasury for your jewels. Allow me to stay, to serve you, to listen to you. Look on me as one of your animals, guarding you faithfully, never leaving your side. What harm could one more do, a slave as young as I? Yet I am one of those crushed by the millstone of love.'

XLVIII

WHEN Majnun heard the stranger's words, the new moon of a smile wandered over his face and he replied:

'Oh, my noble sir! The path you have taken is full of danger and it would be better for you to retrace your steps. Your place is not with me, for you have tasted not one of my countless sufferings. Look, I have nothing left but these few beasts, no foothold of my own—how could I provide one for you? How could I live in harmony with you, when I cannot live with myself? Even demons flee from me and my talk—what then can you hope to gain? You search for the warmth of a human being, but I am a lonely savage. Return to your own kind! Let my story be a warning to you. You and I, we do not agree. Your ways differ from mine; you are your best friend, I destroy myself. Leave me! As a reward for your long journey accept my advice. You have found here one who has become a stranger to himself, one who feeds on pain. Say to him: "Allah be with you!" and leave him as you found him. Go! If you do not leave on your own account, you will in the end have to flee—hurt, soul and body—whether you want to or not.'

Thus spoke Majnun. Salam of Baghdad heard his words, but they did not still his desire.

'I implore you, for God's sake,' he insisted, 'do not refuse my thirst a drink from your well. I have come to you as a pilgrim. Do not prevent me from praying in your Mecca!'

In the end, pressed hard by the youth, Majnun, to his regret, had no choice but to give in to his demand. Salam was happy. Fetching his bundle, he opened it, spread a rug on the ground and heaped delicacies upon it: halwa, sweetmeats and other sugared and spiced food.

Then he said:

'Be my guest, as I am yours! Break bread with me, do not refuse my repast. You may want to fast, but man, according to his nature, must eat to retain his strength. Fall to!'

But Majnun did not accept his invitation. 'I am one of those,' he replied, 'who have eaten the eater within themselves. Bread and halwa feed the strength of those who look anxiously after their own well-being. I am free from this anxiety. How then can fasting harm me?'

The youth from Baghdad took these words in his own way. Thinking that he should encourage and comfort the comfortless, he replied:

'It would be better if you did not always feed the despair in your heart. Even the sky does not remain the same! It changes face and constantly reveals to us new pages in the book of fate. One moment, brief as the blinking of an eye, may open a hundred doors leading from grief to joy. Do not be so faithful to your sorrow; better to turn away from it, better to laugh than to weep, even if the wound still smarts. My heart also was broken, my body exhausted and paralyzed. Yet Allah, in his mercy, showed me the way out of this misery. In the end, your grief too will be softened and you will forget what happened. Is not the flame of love, which set you alight, the fire of youth? When the youth becomes a man, even this burning furnace cools down.'

The advice was well meant; Majnun suppressed his anger and answered:

'Who do you think I am? A drunkard? A lovesick fool, a slave of my senses, made senseless by desire? Understand: I have risen above all that, I am the King of Love in majesty. My soul is purified from the darkness of lust, my longing purged of low desire, my mind freed from shame. I have broken up the teeming bazaar of the senses in my body. Love is the essence of my being. Love is fire and I am wood burned by the flame. Love has moved in and adorned the house, my Self has tied its bundle and left. You imagine that you see me, but I no longer exist: what remains, is the beloved....

'And you believe this love, so heavy with grief, could ever run dry? Never—unless the stars pale in the sky. You think this love could be torn from my heart? I tell you, sooner you could count the grains of sand in the desert!

'Therefore, if you want to talk to me, keep your tongue in check. Rather take care of yourself and spare me such nonsense!'

Thus Majnun advised the youth, who had to admit his error. Beware of thoughtless speech! Before you shoot your arrow, test the bow: is not the string too slack for the target, your arm too weak? Words can be shot even faster than arrows, but shame and regret remain.

Only for a short time did Majnun and the youth from Baghdad walk the same path. Had not the hermit warned his visitor? For a while Salam bravely accepted life in the desert; and not without reward, for Majnun's verses were wonderful gifts, pearls of great beauty, which he, the wanderer through the world, scattered on the ground. Salam collected them all and preserved them carefully in the casket of his memory.

But soon the youth from Baghdad could no longer endure life in the wilderness without food or sleep. He felt that he would perish if he stayed much longer and so he left the beasts and their master, returning to the land of men and to Baghdad. There, he made people listen to the poems he had gathered and all were amazed and moved to the depths of their being.

XLIX

WHATEVER befalls us has its meaning; though it is often hard to grasp. In the Book of Life every page has two sides. On the upper one, we inscribe our plans, dreams and hopes; the reverse is filled by providence, whose verdicts rarely match our desire.

Who can decipher fate's handwriting? However, what at first we are unable to read, we then have to endure later on. Our thoughts and wishes go out into the future, but often we make mistakes and have to pay when our reckonings do not balance. Thus we admire a rose and long to possess it; but a thorn wounds our outstretched hand; it bleeds when we withdraw it. We suffer from hunger and thirst and unfulfilled desire, and forget that satisfaction might be our peril and indigence our salvation.

Often fate and man's desire are in conflict; it is better, therefore, to accept than to rebel. Do not forget that what appears to be vinegar sometimes proves to be honey.

Layla, the enchantress, was a treasure to others, but a burden to herself. If to her husband she appeared to be a precious jewel, he was for her a serpent coiled around her. In his eyes she was the moon; she saw him as a dragon holding her in his jaws. So each suffered from the other.

For Layla this existence was constant torment. Was she not like a ruby enclosed in the heart of a stone? She had no weapons but patience and deceit. She knew no other grief or happiness but her secret love which she hid from all eyes, especially from those of her husband, Ibn Salam. Was he in a better state? Was his fate easier than Majnun's?

In the eyes of the world he possessed Layla, who was more precious to him than anything else; yet this possession was an illusion. He knew this and he too had to keep it secret. He guarded a treasure to which no path would lead him, although it belonged to him; he was not allowed to enjoy what was his.

Such a wound smarts, but his love was so strong that

he felt grateful even for pain. He was a magician keeping a fairy captive in the world of men, to worship her for ever.

Did Layla know that? She hid her tears from her husband. When he came, she smiled. She was like a candle which burns alone, spreading its cheerful light yet shedding waxen tears at the same time....

But the turning wheel of heaven reveals what fate has decided, without pity for mortal man. Where, in the end, is he to go, who loves without being loved? In time Ibn Salam lost all hope. Layla saw him rarely and, estranged from her who, though his wife, was still a bride, he fell ill.

The grief hidden in his soul poisoned his body. A violent fever seized him and his breath was as hot as the wind from the desert.

A doctor was called, a skillful man, who well knew his art. He felt the patient's pulse, examined his water and gave him healing potions which gradually quenched the fire. Thus he showed the ailing body a way to health and it seemed that Ibn Salam was saved.

But as soon as he was slightly better, he ate and drank and did what the doctor had forbidden him. The fever which had sheathed its claws, attacked anew, the evil which had left him, returned.

What was to be done? This time the doctor was

helpless. Thus the first wave of the flood softens the clay, the second carries it away. A wall, cracked and shaken to its foundations, may survive one tremor; if a second wave follows, it must collapse.

Ibn Salam was still young, though weakened by illness and grief. For two or three days his strong nature resisted the new attack, but then his breathing became slower and heavier until the soul fled his body and left this world of misery, dancing away from the earth with the wind.

What we are and possess is but a loan—and that not for long! Do not clutch what has been given to you, for joy and desire to possess are but nails fastening you to the perishable world. To obtain your jewel you have to burst open the casket and take wing like the dove from the tower on which you are standing...

Ibn Salam, then, was dead.

And Layla? What did she do? Although she had never loved him, he had, after all, been her husband and she pitied him. On the other hand—she felt relief. For how long had she veiled her heart like her face! Now she felt like one of the animals, gazelles or wild asses, which her beloved had freed from the hunters' snares: the shackles she had worn for years suddenly fell off.

How she enjoyed this freedom to weep to her heart's content, without shame or fear of watchful eyes. No one could be certain whom she was mourning. No one could know that she was shedding tears not for the dead Ibn Salam, but for the living Majnun. Only the outer shell of Layla's mourning was her husband's—the kernel was her beloved.

Now Layla too was free, as free as Majnun, but her freedom was different. It is the custom among the Arabs that after her husband's death a widow must veil her face, seeing no one; for two years she must live in her tent, withdrawn from the world, mourning and lamenting the dead.

Nothing could be more welcome to Layla. Now she was free, without fear, to give heart and soul to her beloved.

L

AUTUMN had come. In the garden the leaves were falling like drops of blood. The warmth of the sun escaped from rivers and lakes, the face of the landscape became sere and yellow. The flowers shed the color and brilliance of their garments. Ready to depart, the narcissus tied its bundle. The jasmin's silver lost its precious gleam and the rose-petals became a book of mourning. Like sailors afraid of a storm, branches and calyxes threw their load overboard and the gardeners collected apples, grapes and berries to protect them from the advancing winter.

And as the garden fared, so fared Layla. Her spring had faded, withered by the Evil Eye of the world, and her flame flickered in the gusts of the wind. The fairy-one had become weak and transparent; of the full moon only one half remained, and of the proud cypress only its shadow. Our tulip shed her petals!

A cold fever shook her limbs and spread dark blotches and stains over her sweet face. Layla could hardly leave her bed and her soul prepared to leave the body like a pheasant abandoning the crown of the felled cypress tree.

She knew it well. Sensing that death stood close, she allowed no one near but her mother, revealing in this hour for the first and last time, the secret of her love. Then she said:

'Mother, oh my dear mother, how does it happen that a gazelle kid imbibes poison with its mother's milk? I am fading away—and what has my life been? I have suffered so much in secret that now I must talk. Before my soul escapes, the grief in my heart breaks open the seal on my lips. I must draw back the curtain and then I shall go. My beloved, for whom I have lived and for whom I die, is far away. Listen to me, mother!

'When I am dead, dress me like a bride. Make me beautiful. As a salve for my eyes, take dust from Majnun's path. Prepare indigo from his sorrow, sprinkle the rose-water of his tears on my head and veil me in the scent of his grief. I want to be clad in a blood-red garment, for I am a blood-witness like the martyrs. Red is the color of the feast! Is not death my feast? Then cover me in the veil of earth which I shall never lift again.

'He will come, my restless wanderer—I know. He will sit at my grave searching for the moon, yet seeing nothing but the veil—the earth—and he will weep and lament. Then, mother, remember that he is my friend—and how true a friend! Remember that I leave him to you as my bequest! Treat him well, comfort him, never look harshly upon him. Do so, for God's sake, because I have loved him and my wish is that you too should love him as I did.'

But Layla's heart was not yet stilled in her care for Majnun:

'When he comes, mother, and you see him, give him this message from me! Tell him: "When Layla broke the chain of the world, she went, thinking of you lovingly, faithful to the end. Your grief in this world has always been hers and she has taken it with her to sustain her on the journey. The longing for you did not die with her. Behind the veil of earth, you cannot see her eyes, but they are looking for you, following you wherever you go. They are waiting for you asking: when do you come? ..." Tell him that, mother!'

Thus Layla spoke. Tears streaming down her face,

she called the name of her beloved. Then her voice died away and she crossed the frontier into the other land.

When death had closed her lips, the mother's grief was boundless. She tore her jasmin-white hair and embraced and clasped her daughter's body as if she could breathe life into it again. She pressed her face against Layla's forehead and her tears glinted and sparkled like a cluster of stars on the extinct moon.

To no avail—even if heaven itself had joined in the lament. Everyone must cross this threshold, but none returns.

LI

I T happened just as Layla had foretold: when Majnun in the wilderness learned about the death of his beloved he set out at once. He came like a thundercloud driven by the storm and fell down on her grave as if struck by lightning. Do not ask what it looked like, his burnt-out heart!

Enough! People who saw and heard him were so terrified that they fled; some even wept for him. Like a serpent, twisting and turning over the treasure which it guards, he writhed in torment and his tongue was a flaming torch of lament.

'Oh, my flower,' he exclaimed, 'you withered before

you blossomed, your spring was your fall, your eyes hardly saw this world.'

To those who watched, Majnun appeared madder than ever and so did his words, which resounded in their ears, words which he addressed to his beloved in her grave:

'How do you fare where you rest now, down there in the darkness? Your musk-mole, your gazelle eye—where are they? The splendor of your agate lips, the amber-scented coils of your tresses—what has happened to them? Which colors adorn you there, you, my beautiful picture? In what bowl do they melt you, my candle? Whose eyes do you gladden now? On which bank do you grow, my cypress tree? And in which tulip garden do you celebrate your feast? How do you spend your time in the cave? Where there are caves, there also live serpents! Do you not know that? What does a moon like you seek in such a place? Look, I suffer for you and your life in the cave! Or are you a buried treasure now? You are; else you would not have disappeared into the earth. But every treasure has a serpent in its cave to guard it. This guardian am I! I am your serpent, I have no other abode.

'How changed you are! Your fate was clouded, disturbed like sand on a desert path; suddenly you have fallen still, like the water in the depth of a well. Yet, even if you are hidden from my eyes, my heart can see you and will never lose you. Even if your form has vanished—your sufferings here will endure through eternity.'

Then Majnun jumped up again. He was not alone, for his beasts surrounded him in dumb loyalty. Now they followed him back into the wilderness, while he sang of love, which is stronger than death.

Thus the caravan moved through the desert. The sand wept with Majnun, the mountains echoed his mourning songs, his lament struck sparks from the thorn-bushes in the gorges and the stones of the steppe glowed with the color of his blood.

But even the wilderness no longer offered a refuge to this homeless heart. Again and again his longing drove Majnun back to the grave of his beloved; like a mountain stream he rushed down into the valley, covering with thousands of kisses the earth where his buried love awaited him.

While he was lying there, weeping and telling his grief, the animals kept watch over him, so that he should not be disturbed.

Thus it happened that people began to avoid Layla's grave. Not surprisingly, for who was to know whether the madman would suddenly appear? Who wanted to be struck down by a lion's paw, to be torn by a wolf's fangs?

LII

MAJNUN covered the last pages of his book of life with the black darkness of his mourning. He traveled rapidly towards death, but however fast he moved, it still appeared too slow to him. He was a pilgrim in this world, his Mecca a grave, his inn the loneliness of desert and rock. The harvest of his days on earth was burnt and the millstones of heaven were grinding him to dust.

There came a day when he felt a great weakness. Once more he dragged his body to Layla's tomb. When he arrived evening had fallen, darkening the ocean of the sky. Soon Majnun's boat was to weigh anchor for his journey into the night.

He resembled an ant exhausted unto death, twitching for the last time, a serpent writhing in its death-throes. Weeping, he recited some verses; then, his eyes closed, he lifted his face, raised his hands towards the sky and prayed:

'Maker of all things created! I implore thee in the name of everything which thou hast chosen: relieve me of this burden. Let me go where my love dwells. Free me from this cruel existence and, in the other world, cure me of my torment here.'

With these words, Majnun lay down his head on the

earth and embraced the gravestone with both arms, pressing his body against it with all the force he could muster. His lips moved once more, then with the words, 'You, my love...', the soul left his body.

LIII

MAJNUN remained as lonely in death as he had been in life. Having found his rest, he was safe from wagging tongues; for a long time no one knew, no curiosity disturbed his slumber.

Some say that he remained lying on the grave of his love, where he had died, for a month or two. I have also heard that the time was even longer, that as much as a year passed.

People thought him still alive! Whenever they came to watch from afar, they saw wild animals surrounding the grave. Protected by them, Majnun slept safely like a king in his litter. Even now, they did not leave their master, unwilling to believe that he would never awaken again. Patiently they waited and Layla's tomb seemed to have become a home for the roving beasts.

Afraid of such guardians, people did not dare to approach. They thought and said to one another: 'The stranger is lying on the grave as usual.'

Thus the dead man was left alone; even beasts which

feed on carrion did not touch him. What little remained of him fell into dust and returned to earth; in the end nothing was left but his bones.

Then only did the animals abandon their watch; one after the other they disappeared into the wilderness. When the magic lock had been removed from the hidden treasure, people approached to solve the riddle and found what remained of Majnun. Death had completed his work so well that no one felt fear or disgust. The white shell, its pearl vanished, was washed clean and men let jewelled tears of mourning flow into it.

They all wept—members of Majnun's and Layla's tribes, as well as others, strangers of pure heart mourning the lovers, rending their garments in lamentation.

And Majnun was buried at Layla's side.

> *Two lovers lie awaiting in this tomb*
> *Their resurrection from the grave's dark womb.*
> *Faithful in separation, true in love,*
> *One tent will hold them in the world above.*

LIV

Sweet, gallant Zayd never abandoned the grave of our twin fountains of light. Stringing together their candid verses with sensitivity, he exposed Layla and Majnun's *affaire de coeur* to the admiration of the world.

One day a query kindled his imagination. How was that pair of unsated souls faring behind the veil? Had they become brick molded in dark earth or filigree ornamenting the throne of God? When night opened its pouch and scattered musk over the day, in his sleep an angel revealed to Zayd a luminous, many-splendored garden.

Its scenery was exhilarating, with trees lofty as exalted fortune. There was a miniature garden in the lap of every blossom, a shining lamp in every flower petal, and to the seeing eye, a blue empyrean in every meadow. The garden was greener that an emerald, and shone with infinite light. Blooming roses offered up their cups and drunken nightingales raised a clamor. Minstrels plucked their strings as doves cooed the melody of Zand.

In the shade of a solar rose, a divan draped with heavenly brocade had been set up beside a stream. Two angelic beauties were seated in this place of pleasure, arrayed like the houris of paradise in raiments of light. Facing springtide with wine in hand, they were together as in a fairy tale, pressing their lips to their wine cups, and then joining in a kiss. After sharing in conversation, they would repose in their heart's desire.

An ancient soul stood in attendance, showering them with blessings. The dreamer asked him surreptitiously, "Who are these two with figures like cypress trees, bearing cups in the fabled garden of Iram? How have they come to attain their desire in this spiritual abode?"

After a moment, the old man replied, "These two friends are one, eternal companions. He is Majnun, the king of the world in right action. And she is Layla, the moon among idols in compassion. In the world, like unpierced rubies they treasured their fidelity affectionately, but found no rest and could not attain their heart's desire. Here they suffer grief no more. So it will be until eternity. Whoever endures suffering and forebears in that world will be joyous and exalted in this world."

When morning's conflagration consumed the harvest of night, Zayd awoke and revealed the secret of his dream. Whoever would find a place in that world must tread on the lusts of this world. This world is dust and is perishable. That world is pure and eternal. Mind you, do not grant such a thorn that rose. Rise out of the mine, this gem will not be found underground. Commit yourself to love's sanctuary and at once find freedom from your ego. Fly in love as an arrow toward its target. Love loosens the knots of being, love is liberation from the vortex of egotism. In love, every cup of sorrow which bites into the soul gives it new life. Many a draft bitter as poison has become in love delicious. With love for a saqi, what is there to fear from a bitter draft? However agonizing the experience, if it is for love it is well.

Inayatiyya

A Sufi Path of Spiritual Liberty

Sulūk Press is an independent publisher dedicated to issuing works of spirituality and cultural moment, with a focus on Sufism, in particular, the works of Hazrat Inayat Khan and his successors. To learn more about Inayatiyya Sufism, please visit **inayatiyya.org**.